THE
Focus on the Family
Clubhouse
COLLECTION

THE Focus on the Family Clubhouse COLLECTION

A TREASURE CHEST OF STORIES
Edited by Ray Seldomridge

PUBLISHING

Colorado Springs, Colorado

THE CLUBHOUSE COLLECTION

Copyright © 1993 by Focus on the Family

Library of Congress Cataloging-in-Publication-Data

Clubhouse collection / edited by Ray Seldomridge.
    p.   cm.
    Summary: A collection of twenty stories that originally appeared in the
    magazine *Clubhouse*, including "Lost in the Rain Forest," "The Halloween
    That Stunk," and "Ten Miles to the Amen."
    ISBN 1-56179-161-X
    1. Christian fiction, American. 2. Children's stories, American.
    [1. Christian life—Fiction. 2. Short stories.]
    I. Seldomridge, Ray. II. Focus on the Family Clubhouse.
    PZ5.C65   1993
    [Fic]—dc20   92-36520
                                            CIP
                                            AC

Published by Focus on the Family Publishing, Colorado Springs, CO 80995.

Distributed by Word Books, Dallas, Texas.

This is a work of fiction, and any resemblance between the characters in this book
and real persons is coincidental.

Designer: Jeff Stoddard
Cover and interior illustrations adapted by: Alan Flinn
Illustrations for "The Puppy Attack" and "Ten Miles to the Amen"
based on original illustrations by David Slonum

Printed in the United States of America

93 94 95 96 97 98/10 9 8 7 6 4 5 4 3 2 1

Acknowledgements

The stories in this book came about through the dedicated efforts of many people. I wish to thank Dr. James Dobson and Rolf Zettersten for asking me seven years ago to start a children's magazine, Dean Merrill for expertly guiding our editorial work, and Tim Jones — along with his art staff — for making the stories so visually appealing upon first publication.

I'm also indebted to Focus on the Family's Al Janssen, Gwen Weising, Deb Nelson and Jeff Stoddard for making this book a reality.

Most of all, I'm grateful to Marianne Hering for "discovering" many of the fine authors represented here.

Table of Contents

Introduction

When I was 10, I read a story about a boy who discovered a tiny door at the back of his closet. Opening it, he tiptoed down a secret staircase and came out into a strange, wonderful world.

I wanted to go with him! But that was only one of many tales calling me to places far away. When I wasn't in Bayport sleuthing with the Hardy boys, I was on a freighter sailing out of San Francisco with Tod Moran. Or fleeing across the moors of Scotland with David Balfour in *Kidnapped*. I even spent time with Pippi Longstocking and crazy Miss Pickerell, but was yanked away to help out Homer Price in Centerburg when he couldn't shut off the doughnut machine.

Just like world travel, stories are both exciting and dangerous. Dangerous because they can *change* you inside.

God must've known that when He wrote the Bible. He could have given us a long list of do's and don't's or a collection of religious essays. Instead He decided to tell us stories—stories of David and Jonah, Jesus and Paul.

Of course, the stories in this book aren't from the Bible. But many of them *are* about Christian kids trying to follow Jesus. So here's your ticket to join them in 20 different worlds. May your journeys be both exciting *and* dangerous.

Ray Seldomridge

The Puppy Attack

*Several weeks after Angela became mine,
I woke up in the night coughing like crazy.*

by Susan C. Hall

THE PUPPY ATTACK

I wanted, needed, absolutely had to have a dog, but my parents thought of a million reasons for not getting me one. And even though I prayed every night for them to change their minds, I began to think they never would.

Then one evening, as Mom and Dad and I sat in the family room watching television, we heard the sound of thunder.

"Patsy," said Mom. "Please run and close the front door. It sounds like the storm will be here any minute."

Believe it or not, when I got to the door, I spotted a tiny, brown-and-white puppy shivering on our front porch. Quickly I opened the screen and picked it up. Then I raced to the laundry room, where I wrapped it in a warm towel right from the dryer. When the puppy stopped shivering, I unwrapped it and looked it over. I could tell she was a little girl dog, so I decided to call her Angela, the prettiest name I could think of.

"Hi, Angela," I whispered. She wiggled and squirmed and plastered my face with wet kisses. With Angela still in my arms, I headed for the family room, determined to convince my parents that I simply had to have this dog. As soon as Mom and Dad saw Angela, they both grinned.

"I found her on the front porch," I said. "Please, *please* let me keep her. I just know she's meant to be mine."

Daddy nodded. "I think you're right," he said. "Mom

and I have run out of excuses."

Miracles happen, I thought. *They really do. Angela belongs to me—Patsy Allen—the happiest girl in town.*

Angela slept with me every night, which I really loved. But one night, several weeks after she arrived, I woke up coughing like crazy. Then I got a weird feeling in my chest—a sort of tickle and tightening at the same time. Suddenly I could hardly breathe, and I began to make wheezing sounds.

"Mom! Daddy!" I gasped. My parents appeared in a flash. The next thing I knew, we were all at the hospital.

"We called Dr. Bennett," Dad said. "He's going to meet us in the emergency room."

"What's happening to me?" I asked between wheezes. As each minute passed, it grew harder and harder to breathe.

"We'll know soon," said Mom, hugging me to her. "I'm praying that you're going to be fine."

When he arrived, Dr. Bennett gave me a shot. In no time I could feel the horrible tightness in my chest begin to ease, and I started to breathe okay—just like normal.

"What in the world caused all of this?" asked Daddy.

"Patsy's had an attack of asthma," said Dr. Bennett. "It's my guess it was brought on by an allergy. Is there anything different at home—perhaps a new pet or—"

"A puppy," said Daddy. "We have a new puppy, and

Patsy sleeps with it every night."

"That's it," said Dr. Bennett. "Patsy must be allergic to the dog. Sometimes people just develop these conditions. It will have to go."

"No!" I bellowed. "No! No! No!"

Dr. Bennett ignored me and said, "I'm going to keep Patsy in the hospital overnight for observation. In the meantime, you'll have to get rid of the dog and thoroughly vacuum and air out the house."

They took me to a room with a private bed where I cried myself to sleep.

The next morning Dr. Bennett came to see me. I rolled over in bed, turning my back to him.

"Well, the nurses tell me you had a good night, Patsy. No more 'wheezers.'" I could hear him walk over to the bed. He patted me on the shoulder. "I know how disappointed you are about your new puppy, but it can't be helped."

"I want my dog," I said, my back still turned. Dr. Bennett sat down on the bed beside me.

"Look, honey, I'm not going to minimize this. Asthma is a lousy disease. We're going to do some tests to find out if you're allergic to anything else. Chin up, you may well outgrow it someday. Many kids do."

I rolled over and looked at him. "But that's not going to help. Angela needs me now. I need her."

Later, when Mom and Daddy took me home in the car, they told me about Angela. "We found a super home for her," said Mom.

I covered my ears. "I don't want to hear about it."

"Cheer up, honey," said Dad. "We have a surprise waiting for you."

Well, when I got home and saw my surprise, I nearly burst into tears. It was a stupid canary.

"Dr. Bennett told us birds are fine," said Mom. "Isn't it pretty?"

I shrugged.

"What are you going to name it?" asked Daddy. Suddenly everything seemed just too awful to be true.

"Name it? Why would I name a dumb old bird?" I cried and then burst into tears and fled to my room, slamming the door behind me. I started to wail, but even so, I could still hear the canary singing its head off.

I moped around the house all day. That night, I didn't say my prayers. What for? I had prayed for a dog, got it, then had it taken away from me.

I lay in bed for a long time, feeling sorry for myself. Then something occurred to me. The only person I was hurting was me. I needed God now more than ever.

So I prayed after all, asking God to help me learn to live without Angela. Next, I thanked Him for all the good stuff I still had in my life, and it turned out to be a pretty long list. Then I went to sleep.

Next morning the sun streamed through my window and awakened me. I could hear the canary singing again, and I actually felt myself smile.

THE PUPPY ATTACK

Such a cheerful little thing, I thought. I felt guilty that I hadn't even cared enough to give him a name.

Then and there I decided to call him Sunshine.

I still want, need, *have* to have a dog, but I know that, right now, all I can do is hope and pray that I'll outgrow my asthma.

A canary is no substitute for a puppy, but one thing is for sure—that bird can really sing.

Soldier on the Run

Ira just couldn't stand to be bossed around.

by Nancy N. Rue

"**Y**ou have one hour, no more. Then I want you back here tending to your chores."

Court stared at the toe of his boot as his father's words buzzed on.

"It's 1862, son. Everyone has to do his part in this war. Even though you're only 12, your work is important. And son?"

Court looked up into Chaplain Taylor's sternly drawn face.

"Make this your last afternoon wasting time with Private Potter."

If I didn't spend time with Ira Potter, Court wanted to say, *I'd probably go crazy.* But instead he mumbled, "Yes, sir. May I go now?"

There was a sigh for a yes and Court was gone—running out through Fort Churchill's gate, the Nevada wind snapping the flag straight out above his head. No matter what his father had said, Court felt about as significant as the sagebrush his boots smashed as he ran toward the Carson River. *Who could feel important with someone always telling you what to do and whom to be with?*

As the river came in sight through a line of cottonwoods, Court still couldn't see Ira, so he leaned against a tree to catch his breath—and think about yesterday.

When Ira had first made his suggestion, right there on the bank, fear had pounded against Court's ribs.

"You mean go AWOL—absent without leave? Run

away?" Court had asked.

Ira's blue eyes had sizzled at him. "I don't mean turn in a letter of resignation."

Court turned aside so Ira couldn't see his face.

"You know what they do to deserters," Court said.

"Bondage in the guard house, then maybe prison or execution. But that's only if a soldier gets caught."

"But—"

"The minute they discover I'm gone, the bell tolls and they're on my trail. But they'd assume, since I'm an Easterner, I'd head east. Besides—"

Court had watched carefully as Ira pulled out his pocket watch. "If I took off in the midafternoon, four hours before the next muster, I'd be history before they ever knew I'd left."

Court had known of Ira's misery as a soldier for a long time. But yesterday Ira's turmoil had come to a head. "If it weren't for you, I'd go mad," he'd complained to Court. "I hate eating slum gullion, sleeping in a barracks with a dirt floor and making $13 a month, while gents like your papa sit in their big houses drinking imported coffee. And we put up with all this so we can fight a war to guarantee every man freedom and equality. Ha!"

Court had reminded him they were there to guard the Overland Trail from Indians and discourage Southern sympathizers—just as he'd heard his father say.

Ira had told him that was a cartload of hay.

11

But it wasn't until Court had fumed about his own life of "slavery" that Ira had suggested they *both* run away.

The last thing he'd said as he closed his watch was "Two o'clock tomorrow—if you're interested."

L ast night there had been a tangle of voices in Court's head.

His father saying, "Get to those lessons, son. Do your chores. Say your prayers."

Ira saying, "You'll be hearing that till you're 50!"

But after this afternoon's session with his father, when he'd been ordered not even to *see* Ira, there was no more tangle. He was going to pull his own strings now.

Court patted his shirt where he'd stashed several pieces of bread for survival in the Sierras. Then he again searched the bank anxiously for Ira. His friend was never late, especially with that big watch nudging him all the time.

Even as he thought about the watch, Court spotted it, shimmering from a cottonwood branch. He scrambled to the tree, cradled the watch in his hand and opened it. But he already knew what it meant.

The slip of paper inside said:

> Court, I decided I could only take responsibility for myself, not for you. But you've been a friend, and I want you to have this. You'll find your own way to get free.
> I.P.

Court slouched against the tree, whipped by wind and disappointment. Hot tears stung his eyes.

Pressing his back against the bark, he slowly sank toward the ground. "I hope they catch him," he lied aloud to the wind.

The watch said 2:30. Court figured Ira must be no more than three miles away. He put the watch in his shirt and closed his eyes.

By the time Court returned to the compound, the single hour granted him for free time had stretched into four, and he still hadn't decided what to do. The last person he wanted to see was his father.

But in an instant, Court spotted his father's silhouette taking shape in the doorway of their quarters and heard the doleful warning clang of the bell. The sleepy compound came alive with startled soldiers.

"Someone's deserted!"

"It's Potter!"

"A search. There'll be a search!"

Court tried to look surprised, but it didn't matter. No one noticed him except a corporal who barked, "Get back to the house, boy, before you get trampled!"

Almost before Court reached the doorway where Chaplain Taylor stood, hands folded in a white knot in front of him, the horses were being gathered in the compound, and a hundred more shouts mingled with the leaden toll of the bell.

"Alarm!" it clanged. "Soldier gone AWOL."

That message wasn't half as fearful as what Court expected to hear from his father. He knew the struggle he was feeling inside had to be plastered all over his face. *Where have you been, son?* Court imagined the grilling. *You know something, don't you? You knew when there was still time to catch him, and you didn't tell.*

But there was no anger in Chaplain Taylor's eyes when Court got to the door. Even so, Court drew up his shoulders, waiting.

"Private Potter did have choices, Court," his father said.

Court flinched in surprise at his father's words, but he said nothing. *Choices?* he thought. *What choices?*

As if reading Court's mind, his father continued, "He was in a university before the war started. He could have finished and been commissioned as an officer, but he quit. He wasn't willing to work for it."

Court bit his lip.

"He could have made the best of his situation here. *He* knew he was as good as everyone else. He knew it wouldn't last forever."

Court couldn't hold back his words any longer. "Ira isn't the kind of man who can be bossed around!"

He wasn't sure whether he was talking about Ira or himself. His father didn't seem to know either. Chaplain Taylor's profile looked painfully strained. "No matter what kind of man you are, running away is a bad choice."

"But what about all this freedom we're supposed to be fighting for?" Court's voice was desperate. "What about all men being created equal? They aren't, are they?"

His father's hand went under Court's chin, pulling his face up until their eyes met. "I've wondered so often what those words really mean. I don't know, Court—except we *are* equal in God's eyes, and we have to trust that someday He'll even out the score."

They looked at each other for a long moment—until the rifle retort pierced the air in the compound and ricocheted from the walls. Court's head snapped to watch the first column of horses move through the gate, each rider clutching a weapon in front of him.

"Guns!" Court cried. "No!"

He started to bolt, but his father put a hand on his shoulder.

"They won't kill him."

But they'll bring him down, Court wanted to scream. *If I tell them, they'll find him and bring him down. If I don't—*

He looked up at his father, who was watching him closely.

"Court, do what *you* have to do." He sighed. "Maybe that's where the real freedom is. In your own heart, where it's just between you and God."

The bell had finally stopped when Court went up to his room. Ira would know that they'd be searching

15

for him by now. But would he know Court hadn't betrayed him? That the men were heading east because they still didn't know he'd gone west? Or would he be shrinking warily behind every tree—more a prisoner than ever?

Court missed him. But he was glad Ira had not waited for him after all. He shivered at the thought of being trapped into running.

"Good night, Ira," Court said as he got to his knees beside his bed. "I bet even with all the 'Court do this, Court do that' I'm freer than you are, no matter how far you run." Court pulled out the watch, still hidden with the bread rations, and looked at it. "But maybe someday you won't have to hide anymore."

Then he settled down to eat his bread and to talk things over with God.

The California Girl

*Everything about Kim screamed for attention,
so her cousin Mindy got none.*

by Marianne K. Hering

THE CALIFORNIA GIRL

Cousin Kim looked "California." Her hair, her clothes, her voice. Everything about the 12-year-old screamed for attention. And she got it when she invaded Mindy's Idaho home for the Thanksgiving holidays.

First, Mindy's own dog, Clifford, followed Kim around. Then Mindy's mother took Kim shopping. And they didn't go to a lonely K mart or Target; they went to a mall.

Finally, Mindy's father took Kim to a local dog show. Mr.Blake thought she'd like to see the dogs work out. Kim said she wanted a career training animals for the movies.

Ten-year-old Mindy had to stay home and write a report for school about becoming a missionary. But wanting to be a missionary didn't get you much attention. At Mindy's house, you had to be a weird person from California to be noticed.

On the Saturday after Thanksgiving, the Blakes always went skiing. Mindy had to wait over an hour for Kim to finish spraying her hair and caking on makeup.

Once inside the bathroom, Mindy studied the little jars and tubes that Kim had left strewn on the counter. Mystical-mauve eye pencil, royal blue mascara, lemon-mist lotion. *Lemon-scented lotion! That's a perfect fit for Kim,* she thought.

In minutes she had emptied half the bottle and refilled it with lemon juice from the kitchen. After twisting the cap back on, Mindy left the bathroom and went outside to join her cousin, who looked like an alien in a bright, bright pink, yellow and blue ski suit. Then the whole family piled in the van, and Mindy's mom popped in a Christian cassette tape.

Halfway to the ski slope, a Steven Curtis Chapman song was interrupted by Kim's scream. A bug had crawled up the window. Before Kim could squash the creature, Mindy screeched in her ear, "Don't kill it!"

Kim cringed but didn't move. Mindy leaned forward to scoop up the bug with her bare hands and toss it out the window.

"If you were a missionary in the African bush," Mindy lectured, "you'd be thankful for that bug because you might have to eat it for lunch."

Minutes later, the van pulled into the lodge parking lot. On seeing the mountain, Mindy had one mission: to ski down Diablo's Drop *alone*. Gliding down that ultra-steep hill, feeling the wind and being free would make her forget that Kim had ever come.

However, things didn't work out as Mindy planned.

First, her father insisted the girls take the same ski lesson and then stay together "for safety" until lunchtime. After that, the family would ski together.

Next, the instructor paired Mindy with Kim during the class session. (He also kept exclaiming that Kim was "a natural" on skis.) Finally, Kim took Mr. Blake's warning seriously and wouldn't even go to the rest room alone.

However, waiting for Kim gave Mindy her chance to escape.

Since skis were not allowed inside the lodge, Kim took off her long fiberglass boards and propped them in the snow. Once she was inside the building, Mindy picked up her cousin's skis and moved them a few yards—just far enough away so it would take Kim a few minutes to find them. That would be enough time for Mindy to take a chair lift up and away from her California cousin.

Mindy left the lodge and took a chair that met at an intersection of five runs. She decided to practice a bit more before she went down Diablo's Drop. The first run she chose was a beginner's run. She practiced her turns and parallel stopping. The run ended at the lodge, and there stood Kim. Mindy made a sudden turn to stop, spraying snow all over her cousin.

"Someone stole my skis," Kim said, ignoring the snow and staring Mindy right in the eye. "Luckily, our cute ski instructor came by and loaned me some awesome new skis from the rental booth. I guess you got tired of waiting."

Mindy didn't answer.

"The whole ski patrol is looking for my skis," continued Kim. "These loaners are really sweet, top-of-the-line, Rossignol racing skis. They're 170s. Mine were 10 centimeters shorter."

Mindy avoided Kim's stare by studying the new skis in silence. She looked at her own beat-up 150s.

"Oh," Kim babbled on, "and don't use the rest room at that lodge; it's really rank inside. There's slush everywhere, and the lines are 100 miles long."

"Well," responded Mindy, "just be thankful there's a toilet. If you were a missionary in Thailand, you'd have to use a little dirt hole." Mindy looked at the lift, then at her cousin who had the ski instructor and "the whole ski patrol" helping her.

"Come on, let's get skiing," she suggested.

As the girls zipped down the next slope, Mindy noticed that Kim was having trouble with the new skis. They were too long for her, and the tips kept crossing.

Seeing a chance to out-ski Kim and get away, Mindy said, "Hey, let's do Diablo's Drop!"

Mindy and Kim stared down the long, narrow run. Snow hills like mountains erupted across the snow. Patches of ice slicked the sides of the slope. And it was steep. Mindy imagined it went straight down.

"I'll go first," said Mindy as she pushed off. At first she had to snowplow to gain control, but then she began to turn and feel the rhythm of the slope.

At one turn, she looked up and saw Kim start off smoothly. She took the hill fast. Snow flew up at her every turn.

A few turns later, just as Mindy predicted, Kim had fallen into the soft powder. One of her skis slid off a few feet from her before the brakes stopped it. She would be delayed long enough for Mindy to get away.

By lunchtime, Mindy was exhausted from skiing. After leaving Kim, she had taken several runs before skiing Diablo's Drop one last time.

She found her way back to the van at the time appointed to meet her parents. But only her mother was there.

"Kim sprained her ankle on Diablo's Drop," said Mrs. Blake. "She walked halfway down the hill till the ski patrol spotted her. We've got to go pick up Dad and Kim at the first-aid station and go home. Kim needs all of our attention."

Mindy's heart throbbed with anger at Kim for ending the skiing and with guilt for helping it happen. But she felt better when she noticed Kim's old skis on the roof rack. *At least they aren't gone for good,* she thought.

On the ride home the van was too quiet. No bugs crawled on the window. Her mother wasn't listening to Steven Curtis Chapman, and Kim didn't say a syllable about being left alone and injured on Diablo's Drop.

But that night at the supper table, words began to snowball. Kim didn't feel like eating her steak, and Mindy began, "You know, Kim, you'd be thankful for that steak if you were a missionary in—"

"Oh, that's bogus! You don't know diddley squat

about being a missionary," Kim interrupted. "They're supposed to be nice people. Wherever you go, even California, you ought to be thankful if you have any friends at all.

"Friends don't move each other's skis or ditch friends on the slopes—especially not after they've fallen. And friends don't give minisermons every time a person isn't hungry for dinner!"

Everything became a blur for Mindy. Clifford started to bark because of the raised voice. Kim excused herself from the table and hobbled upstairs, banging her crutches against the stairs. Mr. Blake asked Mindy why she had left Kim on the slope, and then Kim screamed from upstairs, "My skin is burning, I can't see!" Suddenly Mindy remembered the lemon juice in the lotion.

It took a long time to sort things out. After Mindy apologized, Kim decided not to go home early. The swelling around her eyes went down after rinsing and a good night's sleep.

But the swelling in Mindy's heart didn't go down as easily. She knew she had acted mean and rotten, yet she still didn't *like* Kim or love her in the way Jesus would want her to.

So she formed a plan. Mindy would befriend Kim and treat her the way she would if Kim were from a different country. Mindy would respect Kim's "California look" with the clothes, earrings and hair spray just as she would a Japanese person's kimono or an Indian woman's red dot on her forehead.

Since Kim wanted to eat healthfully after all the Thanksgiving sweets, Mindy ate cottage cheese and alfalfa sprouts with her.

When Kim wanted to try to train Clifford to moon-walk, Mindy supplied all the dog treats.

A month later on Christmas Day, Mindy knew that she and Kim were friends when she opened the presents sent to her. The first was a ski sweater that Mrs. Blake and Kim had bought the day they went to the mall. And the second was a dead bug. The card read:

For my dear Cousin Mindy who will make a
Super-Cool missionary. Here's your first meal.
Love, Kim

Flame Comes to Town

Maxine wasn't about to take weekly baths
or wear lacy dresses every Sunday.

by Robyn Kundert

FLAME COMES TO TOWN

We crouched low in the thicket. The darkness hid our pursuers from view, while my heart galloped faster than the approaching horses. Their vibration ran from my buckskin boots up to my cowhide hat.

"They're gonna find us, Maxi! You got us into this mess," Caleb accused breathlessly. "Now, how you gonna get us out?"

"Calm down, little brother," I said. "I'll think of something."

"But we're being chased by a preacher and a sheriff!" Caleb sobbed. "If Pa finds out, we'll do chores day and night for a year. It's always this way, Maxi. You get me into trouble, then *I* have to work off most of our punishment just 'cause you're a girl."

"Quiet, Caleb! Let me think."

How *did* we get in this fix? I pondered the events of the past 12 hours.

This morning a ruckus broke out in our small Midwestern settlement. A few townsfolks had invited "Flame" to visit our community. Most people looked forward to her arrival, but some seemed bothered. Emotions stirred as the time drew near for Flame's welcome.

I wanted to be a part of all the action in town, but Pa had a different idea.

"Maxi," he said, "you stay on the farm this morning and help Caleb make soap."

Farming was our main livelihood, but we also had a small business supplying lye soap to the local boardinghouse and general store. My job was to watch the kettle while our household fats and lye boiled together to produce the strong soap.

"But, Pa, please," I said. "I just want to see what Flame is all about."

"Maxine." Pa's voice had begun to rise. And whenever he addressed me as Maxine, I knew I had pushed him to the limit. Pa did not like his authority challenged, and I challenged it plenty.

"When you're done with the soap," Pa continued, "fix yourself up in a dress and act like a young lady."

Determination welled within me as I watched Pa hitch our team of horses and head off to town with Ma. In the pantry was a small supply of lye soap ready to take to the general store. I decided the delivery should be made today, and I set off for town on foot.

The sun glistened high in the sky as I peeked cautiously out the window of Bunker's General Store. Flame was just arriving. In a cloud of steam, she gently swayed into town and positioned herself at the edge of Main Street just past the general store. A large crowd drew to the railroad car like a magnet.

"It's outlandish to have a church in a railroad car," one onlooker commented.

"Her name is Flame; she's a 'chapel car,' " responded another. "Her missionaries have traveled throughout the

Western territory establishing churches. Be hospitable; we invited Flame here."

A knot swelled in my throat. Going to church meant taking a bath every Saturday night, wearing lacy dresses on Sunday and sitting still forever. I decided the presence of Flame in this town wasn't a good idea.

Suddenly a solitary voice rose above the murmurings of the crowd. I strained my neck a bit farther to see.

"Greetings, ladies and gentlemen. I am the missionary for this chapel car, Flame. My name is Parson Wyatt."

The authority in the man's voice quieted the audience for a moment. I took note of the stubbornness in his eyes. Getting this preacher to leave town might take some doing.

"Move on, preacher!" bellowed a voice from the crowd. "We aren't bad folks; we don't need religion here."

"Allow me to correct you," responded Parson Wyatt boldly. "We are *all* sinners, and the price we must pay for that sin is death." Then he launched into his sermon.

As the voice of the missionary swelled, so did the rumble of the crowd.

"But there is good news for you," shouted the preacher. "Jesus chose to die on a cross in your place, rather than live without you forever. Now you can accept Jesus into your heart and live with Him."

"Chug that chapel car to Chattanooga!" interrupted a hostile merchant.

"Bring your wrongdoings to Jesus; He will cleanse and change you—"

The parson's words were drowned in an uproar. Tomatoes and onions hurled through the air, meeting their target on Flame's windows.

"Join the service tonight at 7 o'clock; hear the message and allow Jesus to wash you white as snow," Parson Wyatt concluded. Then he disappeared into the chapel car.

A mischievous scheme began to come together in my mind as I recalled the parson's words beckoning the crowd to be washed clean. I decided to make an appearance at the meeting tonight with a "message" of my own. In the midst of all the Main Street confusion, I slipped quietly back to the farm.

The hour was nearing 7. After accepting a candy bribe, Caleb tagged along reluctantly with me toward town. Pa and Ma thought we were going to the creek to catch bullfrogs.

"I can't believe you're gonna mar a church with soap scribblings," Caleb sighed.

"It's not a church," I reasoned. "It's a railroad car. Besides, scrawling 'PARSON GO HOME!' on Flame will get my message across."

Dusk surrounded us as we approached Flame. Fresh

manure had been dropped on Flame's steps, and tomato pulp stuck to her handrails. I dug a piece of lye soap out of my pocket.

"Caleb," I whispered, "let me climb on your shoulders."

Caleb balanced himself against Flame's side while I climbed up. I peered through the window, scanning the small crowd. Parson Wyatt stood at the podium. Seated directly in front of him was the sheriff, nodding off to sleep. Tucked away in the corner of the last pew were Ma and Pa!

"Why don't you act like other girls?" Caleb murmured. "You should you be home embroidering something."

"Sh-h-h, Caleb. They'll hear us."

Pa threw a sudden glance toward the window. Startled, I jolted away from the light and teetered on Caleb's shoulders. Caleb couldn't balance me any longer. We tumbled in a heap, knocking against Flame with a loud thud.

"It's the troublemakers!" I heard the sheriff exclaim.

Instantly, a stampede of boots pounded across Flame's wooden floor. I scrambled to my feet, dropping the piece of soap. I grabbed Caleb's hand, and we dove for cover in a nearby ditch.

"Everyone stay in Flame," Parson Wyatt shouted. "The sheriff and I will take care of this matter."

They mounted two mares and turned them in our

direction. Hiding was our only option, for we could never outrun the horses. After crawling a short distance in the roadside ditch, we disappeared into a tangled mass of bushes.

That's how we got where we were now. Minutes passed. My cramped legs began forcing me to consider other plans. Then suddenly, pain shot through my arm as I was jerked from my hiding place. My feet dangled in mid-air as the sheriff held me up, eyeball to eyeball.

"No trouble-making kid is going to vandalize a house of God in my town." The sheriff tightened his grip, but set my feet on solid ground.

Parson Wyatt escorted Caleb to my side.

"Who are the young boys?" the parson asked calmly, directing his gaze toward me.

"I'm not a boy!" I answered indignantly.

I expected Parson Wyatt to be spittin' mad, but he seemed unruffled. I gulped hard when he reached into his coat and placed a piece of lye soap in my palm. Was this his way of revealing my guilt to the sheriff?

"I came across this lye today and thought I would use it in my sermon tonight," the parson explained.

Was the lye mine? I didn't really know, but I relaxed a little. Then one of the deputies came and pulled the sheriff away. I guessed I wasn't the only problem the sheriff had to deal with.

Parson Wyatt looked at me again. "Soap can wash away dirt, but it can't change your heart or make it clean."

"If Jesus loves me, why are you talking about changing me?" I shot back.

"Jesus is the only one who can change you on the inside. Why don't you return to Flame with me and hear His story?"

I hesitated. "I know what I did was wrong, and Pa is waiting back there."

"True enough," Parson Wyatt agreed. "But give your pa a chance. Forgiveness not only feels good to receive; it feels good to give away. Nevertheless, disobedience does have its consequences."

"I think she should have to embroider something," Caleb added with a smirk.

"Perhaps you could help me clean Flame," said Parson Wyatt.

"That's a possibility," I agreed. "At least I know where to find the soap."

Note: Although Flame is fictitious, chapel cars were really used from 1891 to 1946.

Secret Formulas

Just when I had Chester Ratfield figured out,
he surprised me.

by Shelly Nielsen

SECRET FORMULAS

After dinner, Willy and I conducted some intensive bug research, which is what future scientists do. We checked under the rocks in Mom's dead flower garden, keeping our notebooks handy in case we came across any interesting specimens. But it was too cold for much activity. The smart bugs had headed for the hills or wherever bugs go in the fall. All that were left were a couple of boring black beetles, and they dove into holes as fast as we uncovered them.

We'd been searching for half an hour before Willy broke the silence: "Hey, Joe. You going to invite Chester Ratfield to your birthday party?"

I almost dropped my notebook.

"Chester Ratfield! Are you *kidding?* Are you out of your mind?"

"Whoa," he said. "I was just asking. Don't get yourself in a twist."

The new guy was the most popular kid in our class. He wore loud T-shirts and flashy tennis shoes. If he liked you, he'd buy the candy bar of your choice right out of the vending machine. Clink, clink, went the coins down the machine chute. Ka-chunk. And there you'd be, munching chocolate. So far he hadn't given me any candy. So far he hadn't given me more than a bored look.

Willy shined his flashlight under a rock. "Maybe Chester Ratfield is just shy."

"Shy! That's a laugh. He's stuck-up."

" 'Expect the best.' That's what my mom says. She says that as Christians, it's the least we can do. I just wondered if it applied to Chester."

I stared at Willy. He looked the same as always. Yellow hair. Freckles. A long, thin mouth that made him look oddly like a frog. But he was talking like a stranger. Wasn't that the way. Just when you thought you knew someone, he went and changed on you. People were like bugs that way. Scratching off their old skins. Crawling out of their cocoons, completely different.

"Forget I brought it up," said Willy. "Think about your new authentic hospital lab coat and chemistry set instead. That should cheer you up."

I smirked. The coat was a birthday present from my uncle the doctor. It was about a zillion sizes too big, but with the sleeves rolled up, it made me look almost distinguished. The chemistry set came from Mom and Dad. It was the present of my dreams, with pellets, powders and mysterious liquids. If you added a drop of green stuff to a mound of crystals in the beaker, it smoked and foamed.

"Come on, Willy," I shouted. "Let's go whip up a formula that'll make the Chester Ratfields of the world disappear. Future scientists of the world unite!"

At lunch later that week, Willy and I staked out a spot at a clean table. Everything was business as usual. Suddenly I felt a nudge against my shoulder. I turned. Chester Ratfield. In the flesh.

"Hey, Joe," he said.

"Hey."

"Buy you a candy bar."

I stared at him, my jaw hanging down to my kneecaps. "Really?"

"Why not?"

"O—okay," I said, picking up my tray. I gave Willy my "this-is-weird" look and followed Chester.

"What kind do you want?" he asked, dropping coins down the vending machine slot. "Anything."

After the big purchase, we took the candy outside and sat on the hill. Down below, the others went on playing volleyball and softball; but they shot jealous looks my way. They'd have traded spots with me in a second. I felt great.

While I finished my peanut butter cup, Chester told funny stories about the other kids in class: Brian Anderson scratched himself an average of twice every minute. Liza Parsons smelled like bacon. Willy White sounded like a dying cow when he sang in music class. It was hysterical. I rolled over on the grass, clutching my stomach.

"Hey, Joe," Chester said, then. "Is it true you got a chemistry set for your birthday?"

"Yeah," I said. "How'd you know?"

"Rumors," he said grinning. "Maybe I could stop over sometime and give you a few pointers. I'm a chemistry whiz. Going to be a scientist someday."

"I happen to be interested in science, too!" I said. "Botany. And Willy—you know, Willy White—is into biology." I imagined the three of us down in the lab, mixing secret formulas. "Sure, come over. Any time. I'm having a birthday party Saturday. Come over then."

"Yeah," said Chester, thinking over the offer. "That'd be great. Listen, I promised I'd shoot baskets with Brian. So I gotta go. Okay? See you." He charged down the hill.

After school I went straight to the kitchen and rummaged through the junk drawer. Finally I found it: the leftover invitations to my party. Very carefully I wrote Chester Ratfield's name on an envelope.

This was the coolest birthday party yet. And the coolest of the cool was Chester Ratfield. He threw streamers. He led the singing of "Happy Birthday to You." And he cracked jokes until we were all falling over. Yes, sir. Birthday parties could make a guy feel like a Hollywood celebrity. I sat back and took it all in.

"Psst," Chester whispered after cake and ice cream. "What about the chemistry set?"

We had to time it so no one saw us leaving. But after Chester slipped out, I followed. We met in the hall. "This way," I said.

We sneaked downstairs in the dark. At the bottom I turned on the light.

"Wow," he said when he saw my set-up. "Where's

the microscope?"

"Don't have one yet. I'm still saving."

"What happens if I mix and this?" Chester sprinkled powder into a flask, then dripped in some liquid. "Ka–Bloom!" he yelled, ducking under the table, scattering test tubes.

The door opened and everyone came crashing downstairs.

"Just a little explosion," Chester explained, emerging from under the table, snickering.

It was total bedlam, everyone grabbing beakers and vials. But fun. Mom had to break it up and herd us all back upstairs.

One by one, kids took off. I was standing by the front door saying so long when I heard Brian Anderson's voice in the kitchen, loud and clear.

"Well you saw the chemistry set," he said. "That's what you came for, wasn't it? What'd you think?"

Chester's voice answered back: "It's not so much. No need hanging around *him* anymore."

Then they came into the living room and we were eyeball-to-eyeball. They took off—fast.

Now the house was quiet.

I went to the kitchen and opened the freezer. I got out the ice cream and scooped a heaping bowl. I added bits of leftover cake and stirred and stirred until I had a nice lumpy batter. It was terrifically gross.

I took my bowl to the table and sat down. *All right*, I

thought. *Approach this scientifically*. Here were the facts: (1) Chester was not my friend until he discovered I had a chemistry set. (2) Then his outlook changed overnight. (3) He pretended to be my friend just to get at it. (4) He was a jerk. (5) I was an idiot.

Willy came in, his arms full of rumpled wrapping paper. He dumped everything in the garbage and pulled up a chair. "So I was wrong about Chester. Even scientists make mistakes. Forget about him. How about some bug research?"

I wolfed down the rest of my ice cream, then we took the notebooks and our insect identification book and went outside into the cold. We worked silently, side by side. *We'll be great scientists someday*, I thought, *because we have what it takes. Concentration—dedication—and brains.* That was more than I could say for Chester the Rat.

Mom came to the door and hollered, "Hey, birthday boy! Phone's for you."

I dashed to the phone, thinking Grandma might be on the line.

But it was *him*. Chester.

"I just wanted to say . . ." He paused. "Sorry. I didn't mean what I said. I'm sorry. I mean, I didn't mean to . . ." He stuttered around for a while and then was quiet.

I clutched the phone in my sweaty hands, praying silently, "God, help me forgive him." I let out my breath. "It's okay, Chester." Then I added, "See you Monday."

Outside Willy was still at it. I picked up the notebook I had tossed into the grass. What this situation needed was a scientific analysis. *Chester Ratfield* I wrote at the top of my notebook. But for once I didn't feel like analyzing anything. Just when I had someone pegged, he surprised me. People were like that. Maybe I'd just wait and see . . . expecting the best.

Lost in the Rain Forest

A notebook containing valuable Bible translation work is missing somewhere in the South American jungle. It's up to you to find it.

by Ray Seldomridge

LOST IN THE RAIN FOREST

You awake before dawn, disturbed by the clicking and whirring of the FAX machine. A message drops into the wire cage. It's from mission headquarters:

> PROFESSOR ROBBINS HAS BEEN ATTACKED AND KILLED IN THE JUNGLE BY UNKNOWN TRIBESMEN. HIS NOTEBOOK, CONTAINING YEARS OF TRANSLATION RESEARCH, IS PRESUMED LOST OR STOLEN. IT MUST BE RECOVERED, OR ELSE THE CUJARHUA TRIBE WILL HAVE TO WAIT AN ADDITIONAL SEVEN YEARS FOR A BIBLE IN THEIR LANGUAGE. GOD GO WITH YOU.

You ask the Lord for His strength and guidance. Then you splash cold water on your face, gulp down some oat bran, snatch your backpack and charge out of the apartment.

If you decide to drop into the jungle via helicopter, *go to 1.* If you rent a motorboat, *go to 7.* If you plan to hike in, *go to 18.*

1 The copter lands on a terraced mountainside covered with the ruins of an ancient Indian civilization. You jump out and hike downslope into the jungle below. The air is hot, heavy and swarming with mosquitoes. You spy more ruins in the jungle not far away. But you hear a scream from the opposite direction. If you decide to explore the ruins, *go to 8.* If you follow the scream, *go to 10.*

2 You made it! *Go to 21.*

3 The sandy streambed at the bottom of the chasm cushions your fall. But a flash flood rushes down upon you, snatches you up and carries you for what seems like miles. It stops as quickly as it started, and you lay there totally exhausted and discouraged, asking God if you may give up the search for the notebook. Dusk is coming on. Your despair is made complete when a bloodcurdling screech rends the air. You groan, feeling unable to face another challenge. *Go to 13.*

4 You come across a trail. To your left, the path seems to head toward a cliff. To your right, you spot something blue lying near the trail. If you try to head left, *go to 15.* If you head right, *go to 17.*

5 The butterfly leads you through 6-foot-high periwinkles. Because of them, you do not see the embankment, so you fall headlong onto a sandy beach. Not far away, an abandoned rowboat is tied up at river's edge. You free it, climb in and push off downstream. *Go to 16.*

6 When you mention the name "Robbins," the tribesmen lower their weapons and grin widely, showing their decayed teeth. Obviously Professor Robbins was their friend. These people are the Cujarhua, among whom he lived. They are angry about finding him dead,

but since they do not seem to know what happened to his notebook, you decide to move on. If you turn back the way you came, *go to 15.* If you walk out the other end of the village, *go to 24.*

7 The Tamaca River and its branches flow through hundreds of miles of rain forest. But you'll probably never get far, because the boat's motor has something wrong with it. You listen as it coughs and dies. Aided by your rowing, the boat soon brings you to the first of countless forks in the river. The left branch seems to be flowing swiftly and promises to take you deep into the jungle without further delay. The right fork meanders off in a more leisurely fashion. If you decide to go left, *see 12.* If you choose the right fork, *go to 16.*

8 Coming upon some ancient Indian ruins, you begin to study the drawings carved in stone. Suddenly you discover a long, dark passage between the rocks. Lighting a match, you edge through the tunnel. After many turns, you come to a room with a stone altar in the center. On top of the altar is a black, shiny object. Could it be the Professor's notebook? If you reach for it, *go to 22.* If you hesitate, *go to 14.*

9 While standing there, you are nudged on the behind by a 700-pound tapir! Next thing you know, you're falling. *Go to 3.*

10 You come to a roaring river and see a middle-aged woman, with a safari hat and thick glasses, pinned against the river embankment by a herd of peccaries (wild pigs) with enormous tusks. To your amazement, the peccaries seem afraid of you and rush into the river where they immediately drown. The woman thanks you, but her smile turns to a scowl when you explain you are a missionary. She says she is an American anthropologist studying native cultures, and she resents your attempts to change people's religious customs. Using Scripture if possible, what answer do you give her? Say it out loud, then *go to 20*.

11 Congratulations! You have remembered to call upon the Lord for help in time of trouble. As you do so, a school of piranha—in the hundreds—attacks the snake, and it lets go of your boat. You quickly row ashore. *Go to 4*.

12 White water is dead ahead. And there in the midst of the turbulent river is a man flailing his arms and sinking under the foam. With an oar you steer toward him and grab his collar. You somehow pull him aboard and work your way to shore, where you build a campfire. While pulling off his soggy business suit, the man explains that his purpose in coming to the rain forest was to survey it for commercial development. "Big money," he drawls, "is the only thing that could get *me* to visit this stinking swamp!" What do you reply (using the Bible, if possible)? Say it to him, *then go to 19*.

13 Glancing up in alarm, you make out the form of a howler monkey swinging through the dark limbs overhead. You struggle to sit up, but your motion apparently startles the creature. A rock-like object plummets out of the sky and hits you square on the head. Minutes pass before you regain consciousness. In the dim light, you spy something lying at hand. It can't be—but it is! The Professor's notebook! The monkey must have dropped it. By now the screeching and chattering is all around you. Toucans have joined in yelling; invisible parrots are squawking. Every creature in the forest seems to be having a good laugh at your expense. Grinning, you lift your weary body and begin your trek back to the civilized world.

14 Your match burns out, and it's too dark to find another. As is your custom, you get encouragement by quoting the Bible: "My God turns my darkness into light" (Psalm 18:28b, NIV). You grope along the black passageway until daylight finally appears in the distance. Emerging from between two stone columns, you are amazed at the sight of a giant butterfly winging through the trees. If you decide to follow it, *go to 5*. If, instead, you want to investigate a strange roaring noise, *go to 10*.

15 You come to a deep, narrow chasm. You catch a glimpse of something flat lying on the ground on the other side. If you grab some strong vines overhead to try swinging across, *go to 2*. If your courage fails and you stall, *go to 9*.

16 You fail to notice the giant anaconda that has begun wrapping itself around your boat. You cry out; this snake must be 30 feet long and is certain to strangle you! If you panic and try to fight it off with your brute strength, *go to 23*. If you try something else, *go to 11*.

17 It's the bluish plaid hat you've seen Professor Robbins wear! The attack must have occurred here. Continuing down the trail, you enter a tribal village with thatched longhouses. Immediately you are surrounded by angry warriors—some armed with bows, others with blowpipes and darts. Their leader addresses you in a strange language. You try to describe, mostly with gestures, who you are and whose notebook you are looking for. Do it now, then *go to 6*.

18 You rent a jeep and roar down the steep, narrow streets of Cuzontos, then out into the grainfields. Soon you come to a dead-end loop at the jungle's edge. You climb out of the jeep, sling on your backpack and forge under the dark canopy of trees. *Go to 8*.

19 The man looks at you like you're weird. By now, his clothes have dried, so he puts them on and stumbles away—right into a column of army ants! The column is at least half a foot wide and stretches as far as the eye can see. Swatting and cursing the ants on his pant legs, the man eventually disappears. If you get back into the boat, *go to 16*. If you strike off into the jungle, *go to 4*.

20 The woman isn't interested. After mumbling something about "two missionaries in one month," she disappears into a bamboo maze. You begin looking around and spot an abandoned canoe at river's edge. You climb in and begin to row. The river divides. If you choose the left fork, *go to 12*. If you choose the right fork, *go to 16*.

21 At your feet is a flat, shiny object. You stoop to pick it up. Ah! It's only a piece of slate—the kind of rock used by the natives to make arrowheads. A sudden clap of thunder and outburst of heavy rain catch you off guard. The ground turns to slippery clay. You lose your balance and fall feet first into the chasm. *Go to 3*.

22 You realize too late that the object is not the missing notebook, but a carved idol. Before you can even quote, "You shall have no other gods before me," the floor gives way. Dropping the idol, you plunge down a dark chute into a rowboat on an underground river. Stunned, you lay back as the boat glides through a maze of dark tunnels to the outside. Before you can paddle to shore, the river divides. If you head down the left fork, *go to 12*. If you take the right fork, *go to 16*.

23 Fool! You've forgotten that your only real strength is that which God can give you. The anaconda drags you into the water. Quick—recite a Bible verse in which someone calls on the Lord for help or tells how powerful He is. (Look one up, if you have to.) As soon as you do, a school of piranha—in the hundreds—comes along and attacks the snake for the prize of your flesh. In the confusion, the anaconda lets go. You scramble into the boat and row ashore. *Go to 4.*

24 The trail seems to lead up to a chasm. Starting to turn back, you reconsider when you catch sight of a flat object lying near the edge. You decide to check it out. *Go to 21.*

The Missing Notebook

*What if Mrs. Galbreath found the horrid sketch
that Tanya had made of her?*

by Paul McCusker

Tanya Sanders scowled. She'd been sitting in English class minding her own business when Mrs. Galbreath, the teacher, started asking her questions she didn't know the answers to.

Once, kids even laughed at her. *Who cares about Mark Twain?* she muttered to herself. *And why does Mrs. Galbreath keep picking on me?*

Tanya lowered her head and scribbled furiously in her red-covered notebook. She often doodled when she felt emotional about something. Whole gardens would appear on her papers when she felt happy, teardrops and frowning faces when she was sad, and hideous monsters when she was angry.

This time, the random lines began to resemble a distorted, grotesque cartoon of Mrs. Galbreath herself. Underneath this caricature, Tanya wrote "Mrs. Gallbladder." She tilted it just enough for Jessie, her friend one seat over, to see. Jessie's eyes widened, and she had to cover her mouth to keep from laughing.

Mrs. Galbreath turned from the blackboard and cast a reproving glance in Tanya's direction. Tanya nonchalantly closed her notebook and placed it on the shelf under her seat. The bell rang for lunch. Tanya scooped up her books and dashed out of the room with the rest of the class. Jessie caught up with her. "One day you're gonna get in trouble," she teased.

Tanya shrugged it off.

It wasn't until near the end of lunch, when Tanya returned to her locker, that she realized her English notebook was missing. She tugged at a strand of her curly red hair and recalled her every step. Did she have the notebook when she left class? No. And then she remembered putting it under her seat. She gasped. What if Mrs. Galbreath picked it up and saw the awful picture?

Tanya dashed back to the classroom. The door was closed; the lights out. She stood on her tiptoes to peek through the small window. Tanya saw her desk chair, but the shelf beneath was empty. What had happened to the notebook? Did Mrs. Galbreath have it in her hands at that very moment?

"Can I help you?" a deep, rich voice asked. It belonged to Mr. Jackson, the school janitor.

"I was just looking for a notebook," Tanya explained.

"Red cover?"

"Yeah!" she replied, her hopes beginning to rise.

Mr. Jackson nodded. "Yep, I saw it and put it straight into Mrs. Galbreath's mailbox in the office, since she's on her break."

Racing to the school office, Tanya skidded to a halt in front of the door and straightened up to look as casual as possible.

Behind the counter, Miss Clark, the school secretary

who always had her hair tied up in a bun, smiled at her. "Need some help?"

"Um . . . maybe," Tanya stammered as she trained her eye over toward the wall of teachers' mailboxes. They weren't mailboxes, really, just cubbyholes where papers and letters were placed. She spotted Mrs. Galbreath's box.

Empty!

Tanya groaned, then turned to Miss Clark who had been watching her. "Where is Mrs. Galbreath's mail?"

"Why do you ask?"

"Because I lost my notebook and thought Mrs. Galbreath might have it."

"Oh, yes . . . red cover, right?" Miss Clark said, then explained that Mrs. Galbreath went to the dentist during her break and instructed the secretary to put her mail on her desk in the classroom. "I'm sure she'll give it back to you when she returns."

"I'm sure she will," Tanya called as she dashed out the door. "Thanks!"

Tanya stared at the closed door. *Is it locked?* she wondered as she reached for the handle. *If not, will I get in trouble for sneaking around a classroom I'm not supposed to be in?*

Of course I will! she answered herself even as she turned the handle. It clicked gently. Tanya pulled the door open and slipped into the room. She moved to

Mrs. Galbreath's desk, her eyes searching the surface. There it was beneath the stack of letters and forms! Tanya looked around, already feeling guilty for touching a teacher's desk without permission. *Lunch break is going to end any second now,* she thought. *I must hurry!*

She reached for her notebook, clamped it between her fingers and pulled quickly. Success! Tanya tucked her notebook under her arm and turned to leave.

Somebody coughed.

Principal Myers took Tanya back to his office and left her sitting for an eternity while he disappeared through another door. At long last, the door opened and in stepped Mrs. Galbreath, clutching Tanya's notebook. *Has she looked inside?* Tanya wondered. *Has she seen the picture? Do they expel kids for this kind of thing?*

Mrs. Galbreath leaned against the principal's desk and folded her arms. Her brow was deeply creased. "What were you doing at my desk, Tanya?"

Tanya decided that honesty—or part of it—would be the best policy. "I left my notebook in the classroom, and it wound up on your desk. I wanted it back. That's all."

"Why didn't you wait until I returned?" Mrs. Galbreath inquired.

"I . . . I wanted it for my next class."

"You needed your English notebook for science class?"

Tanya stammered, "Yeah. I . . . I needed the paper."

The lie had a sour taste as she swallowed it.

"Oh," Mrs. Galbreath said, then handed Tanya the notebook. "Here you are. But please don't ever do something like that again. There's been a rash of small thefts at the school, and you look rather suspicious sneaking around. Understand?"

Relieved, Tanya nodded.

"Go on to your next class, and I'll see you tomorrow," Mrs. Galbreath said.

And that was it. No mention of the drawing. No lecture. No punishment. Tanya was free to go.

Fifteen minutes before the bell rang for the end of school, Tanya became bored in her math class. She picked up her red notebook and casually flipped it open in search of the troublesome drawing.

It wasn't there.

When class finally ended, Tanya didn't speak to her friends in the hallway. All she could think about was *Mrs. Galbreath saw my drawing.* She drifted from her locker and out the door to go home, knowing she wouldn't have a very good night. How could she face Mrs. Galbreath in class the next day? What would she say?

In the school parking lot, she stopped dead in her tracks when Mrs. Galbreath, standing next to a large blue sedan, called her name.

This is it, Tanya thought. *My life is over. Mrs.*

Galbreath will flunk me, and my parents will lock me in my room for the rest of my life. She cautiously moved to Mrs. Galbreath's car.

"Hi," Tanya gulped.

Mrs. Galbreath smiled sadly, reached into her pocket and pulled out a neatly folded piece of notebook paper. "If you're angry because I make you think when you're in my class," she said, "then this is worth it. If I make you angry for other reasons, then I'd rather you talk to me about it than take your anger out on your poor notebook. All right?"

Tanya shuffled uncomfortably. "Yes, ma'am," she said softly as she took the folded paper. Her cheeks burned.

"Good." Mrs. Galbreath opened her car door. "That's all I wanted to say."

Tanya stepped away from the car and watched silently as Mrs. Galbreath got in, closed the door and started the engine. It roared to life.

"We're not really monsters, you know," Mrs. Galbreath said with a curious smile through the window. She then put the car in gear and slowly drove off.

Tanya unfolded the piece of paper for one last look at the artwork that had caused her so much grief. But just below the terrible cartoon she'd drawn of Mrs. Galbreath, Tanya found a near-perfect sketch of herself, with Mrs. Galbreath's signature. Startled, Tanya looked up in time to see Mrs. Galbreath wave good-bye.

A Student of the Game

*Whenever they chose up sides,
Johnny was picked last.*

by Susan C. Hall

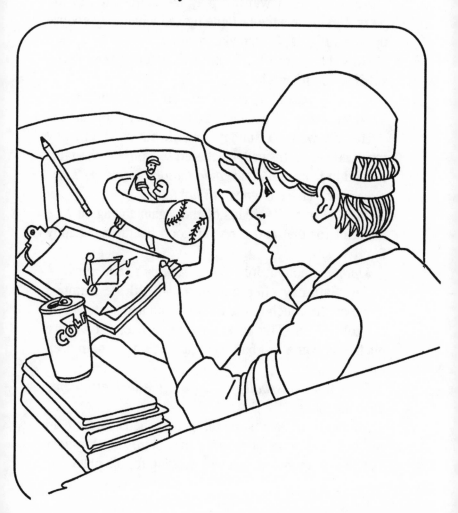

Every night, when Johnny prayed to God, he said the same thing.

"Dear Lord, please make me bigger and stronger and more powerful. I want to play baseball, but I'm too puny. I'm always the last one picked when they choose up sides. *Please*, God, make me grow."

Now 11 years old, Johnny Clausen was still the smallest kid in his class.

"So why pray?" he asked himself. "It doesn't help." Then and there, he decided to quit praying altogether.

He still went to Sunday school, but he didn't pay much attention. Instead, he chased self-pitying thoughts around in his head. *How could God be so mean? Little guys never have a chance. It's not fair.*

"You're smart," said his mother again and again. "Be thankful for that and for your good health and happy family. . . ."

Mothers, thought John. *They just don't understand.*

One Saturday afternoon in mid-April, he slumped down on the couch in the family room and switched on the television. The screen came to life, showing a pitcher deliver a fast ball. He felt the familiar pain deep inside him.

Big-league baseball players are the luckiest people alive, he thought.

Suddenly he saw something that made him sit up straight. A guy about the size of a sturdy sixth-grader had picked up the bat and was heading for the plate.

"The new rookie, Ty Baker, is stepping into the batter's box," said one of the TV announcers. "You know, this kid looks good to me. He isn't very big or strong. He's not going to hit a long ball, but Ty consistently makes contact and gets on base."

"I agree," said a second announcer. "He's an outstanding fielder, too. Always makes the correct play. Baker is what I call a smart ballplayer. A real student of the game."

Small? thought Johnny. *Smart? A student of the game? This could be me.*

He began to read about baseball and to study what the professionals did on the field. He soon realized that the TV announcers' comments were helpful. Lots of these guys had been players themselves. They knew the game well, and John hung on their every word.

For the price of a Popsicle, he could get his sister to pitch to him. Katie wasn't great, but her pitches let him practice swinging the bat and meeting the ball. He spent hours throwing a tennis ball at a chalk target he'd drawn on the fence. It helped improve his aim and strengthened his arm.

He went over plays in his head, thinking what he would do in every situation he could imagine. And when it came time to try out for a position on the Giants, Johnny was there.

The Giants were a church-sponsored team with one of the best coaches in the league, Mr. Peterson.

Unfortunately, Coach Peterson always seemed to be looking at other players when Johnny hit a single or made a good play in the field.

At the outset of the first game against the Royals, John sat on the bench.

"You guys who aren't starting needn't worry," said Coach Peterson. "Everyone on my team gets to play."

The game wore on, and except for Johnny, all the non-starters had gotten into the game.

In the top of the last inning, the Royals scored a run to pull ahead by one. Then in the bottom half of the inning, the first Giant at bat hit a triple. The Royal coach promptly took out the pitcher, substituting a guy named Thomas.

"A hit or a long fly ball will tie this game," cried Coach Peterson.

Unfortunately, Thomas struck out the next two Giant batters.

"Coach?" said Johnny in a small voice. "I haven't had a chance to play yet."

The frantic look that crossed the coach's face stabbed Johnny in the heart. Then suddenly Coach Peterson smiled.

"You're right, Clausen. You'll substitute for the next batter. McDonald follows you. He's our best hitter. Maybe you can draw a walk. *Whatever you do, don't swing at the ball.*"

Johnny picked up a bat and trudged to the plate,

humiliated by his assignment. He stepped into the batter's box, and Thomas wound up and threw.

"Strike one," barked the umpire.

There's no way I'm going to be able to draw a walk, thought John. *This pitcher's too good.* Then John had an idea.

Thomas threw again. Johnny squared around and laid down a bunt along the first-base line.

No one expected it. For a moment the Royal infielders seemed paralyzed by surprise. Then the pitcher, catcher and first baseman all raced to the ball. Thomas got there first, but he had no one to throw to since the first baseman and catcher were right beside him. The runner scored easily from third, and Johnny was safe at first.

The crowd roared.

That ties it, thought Johnny. *If I can get to second base, I'll be in position to score the winning run.* He took a big leadoff, and Thomas fired the ball to first base in a pick-off attempt. Johnny got back safely.

Then Thomas turned his attention to McDonald, who now stood in the batter's box.

Thomas' first pitch was a called strike.

He dropped his chin just before he threw that pitch, Johnny said to himself. *He didn't do that when he tried to pick me off. When I see that chin go down, I'll know he's going to the plate with the ball, and I can take off.*

John pulled off the steal to second like a seasoned pro.

On the next pitch, McDonald sent a line drive to right field. Johnny took off with the crack of the bat, racing for third. He could see Coach Peterson wheeling his arms.

"Keep going, Clausen. Keep going! Keep going!"

Johnny rounded third and headed for home, scoring the winning run.

McDonald got a lot of the glory for hitting the winning run, but Johnny got his share, too.

"Your idea of bunting was smart, Clausen," said Coach Peterson. "Daring, but smart. Where did you learn to bunt?"

"Listening to the sportscasters, watching ball games, reading, practicing," said John. "See, you can't jab at the ball when you bunt. You just have to meet it with the bat. . . ." Johnny stopped and turned red. Who was he to explain bunting to a baseball coach?

But Coach Peterson grinned. "You showed me some fine baserunning, too, my friend. Good job. I'm going to watch you more carefully during practice. Maybe I'll try you at shortstop. We'll see."

By midseason, John had won the job as starting shortstop. But the greatest thrill of the summer came the day he overheard Coach Peterson talking to another coach.

"My little shortstop is the best in the league. He fields the ball well, makes accurate throws, and when he gets to bat, he consistently gets on base. Clausen's a smart ballplayer. A real student of the game."

Johnny began to pray again, but he no longer pleaded to be big, tall and powerful. There were more important things to pray about, and being thankful for the good stuff in his life topped the list.

Cave-In!

Megan knew she shouldn't go into the mine, but how else would her father recover his lost prize?

by S. Jones Rogan

CAVE-IN!

"The mine is dangerous, Megan Roberts," said her father. "'Tis no place for youngsters. Now don't ask to go underground again."

"But Thomas is allowed," pleaded Megan.

"Your brother is 13 and old enough to earn his living down there. You, however, must forget the mine."

Megan's father continued to polish his new Davey lamp. Megan watched the brass glint in the firelight as he worked. "It's a beautiful lamp, Da," she said.

"Aye, lass. Twenty years I've worked in Bendall's slate mine here in Wales; that's about twice your age. They showed their appreciation today when they gave me this Davey lamp. Look . . .'Presented to Owain Roberts, May 12th, 1910.' " He traced the inscription with his finger. "It's special all right."

"Thomas told me there's a massive cavern with an emerald lake in the middle," said Megan, trying one more time.

Da sighed. "I've seen many men injured down the mine, and some die. Please, don't ask again. Hang the Davey lamp over the fireplace. I'll show the lads at work tomorrow."

Megan's father was right about the danger. The next afternoon the dreadful toll of the warning bell sounded. A tunnel deep inside the slate mine had caved in. The anxious eyes of women and children searched the crowd of spluttering miners as they stumbled from the tunnel entrance.

"Da!" Megan spotted her father helping an injured man.
"We're fine, lass. Me and Thomas. Go and tell Mam."

That evening, Megan learned her father's special lamp had been lost in the panic. "I'm sorry, Da," she said. "And you worked all those years."

"Lives are more important," said her father. "Thank the Lord none of *them* were lost."

When Megan climbed the stairs for bed, she overheard her mother. "Is it true, Owain? They'll not reopen the tunnel?"

"Aye, Mam. They'll be jobs lost. At my age, mine be one of the first. Things will be bad with just Thomas' wages."

"Pity about your lamp, Owain. I know it meant a lot to you."

Megan slipped into her brother's room.

"So the rumors are true," said Thomas when Megan told what she'd heard. "I never thought. . . . Poor Da."

"Maybe if we found his lamp, he'd feel better."

"Sure," Thomas scoffed. "And Da would tan my hide for taking you down the mine."

"He needn't know it was us. We'll leave it on the doorstep. We could sneak down after chapel on Sunday."

"I'll think about it, Megan."

She smiled. Thomas always said "I'll think about it" when he liked an idea.

CAVE-IN!

That Sunday, after chapel, they ran to play in the woods. "Come on. Quick!" whispered Thomas.

Megan hitched up her Sunday-best skirts and darted through the trees with Thomas. They climbed the hillside to the gaping, black mouth of the mine entrance. Thomas uncovered two miner's lamps he'd hidden the previous day. He lit the lampwicks and handed one to his sister.

Megan was breathless with excitement. They followed the tunnel deep into the mountain. She shivered and drew her tweed shawl tight around her shoulders. "It's so chilly . . . illy . . . illy," Megan's hollow voice echoed back from the darkness.

"Some tunnels stretch to the other side of the mountain," said Thomas. "Now they're *really* cold."

"How can you work all day with only the lamplight?" asked Megan. "It's so gloomy."

"You get used to it," said Thomas. "They say the whole mine will close soon; the good slate's almost finished. Then I'll work the coal pits in South Wales. They're supposed to be worse."

"You mean, leave home?" asked Megan.

"Da's too old to get another job, so someone has to earn the money."

Before Megan had a chance to reply, the tunnel opened into a tremendous cavern. Megan squinted as a beam of bright sunlight poured through an over-

70

head air shaft and warmed her face.

An emerald and blue mass spread before them. Not even a ripple disturbed the eerie lake. "It's beautiful!" gasped Megan.

"The minerals in the slate make the water that color. And my behind will be the same color if we're caught," said her brother. "Hurry."

They followed one of several passages leading from the cavern. Soon they were stepping over rocks and broken timbers from the cave-in. The air smelled stale, and rivulets of water trickled down the cold rock walls.

"Look around here as quick as you can," said Thomas. "And don't make a sound." They searched in silence. There was no sign of their father's lamp amongst the rubble. The damaged roof supports creaked. "Let's go, Megan. It's not safe."

"Wait. Over there! Something flashed."

Thomas moved the rocks by the wooden timber. "Here it is!" He held up the dented brass lamp. "I hope Da can fix it."

Suddenly, a rumbling shook the ground. "Cave-in!" Megan heard Thomas shout above the noise. "Run!"

Megan fled back to the lake. Thomas wasn't behind her. Megan's heart beat wildly. She trembled all over as she edged back down the dusty tunnel. "Thomas?"

"Here," groaned a voice.

She stumbled over the debris to reach his side. A large timber pinned her brother down. "Oh, Thomas! I can't lift it."

"Get help."

"But I don't know the way," Megan cried. "Which tunnel leads outside? Thomas?" But Thomas didn't answer. He was unconscious.

At the lake, Megan sank to the water's edge. She could be lost for hours following the wrong tunnel from here. Worse still, Thomas could die. Megan stared blankly at her ruined Sunday-best clothes.

Only a few minutes had passed since they first entered the cavern. But now the lake looked like cruel, hard steel as the sun's rays began to fade from the overhead shaft. Megan shuddered. The dwindling rays touched her tear-stained face.

"That's it!" she cried, scrambling to her feet. "The sun was in my face when we came here."

Spotting the only tunnel entrance that was half-bathed in sunlight, Megan hurtled through it. A dot of light appeared ahead and soon became the world outside. She heaved on the warning-bell rope until the villagers came running.

"Megan!" It was her father. "What's wrong?"

She told him about Thomas. "Go home," he ordered.

"Oh Mam," Megan sobbed in her mother's arms. "I wish *I'd* been hurt, not Thomas. Now there'll be no wages at all. We'll end up in the workhouse."

When at last Da returned home, his face was grim.

"We are lucky. Thomas escaped with a broken leg. Megan, you could both have been killed." He held up the battered Davey lamp. "This would never replace you."

Megan's face burned. She lowered her eyes.

"Owain Roberts!" A neighbor pounded on the kitchen door.

"Whatever's the matter?" yelled Megan's father as he stepped over to open it.

"Thomas' cave-in uncovered a new seam. They're going to reopen the tunnel."

"There's no new slate in there, I know."

"Not slate, Roberts. Gold! It uncovered a seam of gold."

"Da!" said Megan. "There'll be enough work for you, and Thomas won't ever have to leave."

"Aye. Thanks be for that. But don't think I've forgotten your disobedience, my lass."

Megan's smile faded.

"No playing after chapel for a month. And here, I want this to sparkle before bedtime." Her father handed her the dirty brass lamp.

"Oh, Da!" Megan grinned.

A Gift for Aunt Rose

*I had to show her that being blind
didn't make me helpless.*

by Susan Cook

A GIFT FOR AUNT ROSE

$\mathbf{T}$ he front door closed with a thud, and I breathed a sigh of relief. I was lying in bed fully dressed and faking a headache, hoping Aunt Rose would go to town without me. It was hard to get her to leave me—the "blind girl from out of town." But her birthday was coming up, and I had to go alone to buy her a gift.

Now that she was gone I had to hurry! Flinging the blankets aside, I took my money and my dark glasses and headed for the kitchen door. It wasn't easy being blind in a new house, but after two weeks it was familiar enough that I could move quickly without bumping into furniture. At the kitchen doorway, though, my foot hit something heavy and soft.

"Francis, you stupid cat! One of these days . . . !" Aunt Rose's huge cat loved to sleep in the kitchen doorway. More than once I had nearly fallen and squashed him flat.

Grabbing the spare key from the hook by the door, I slipped outside. I followed the back fence with my fingertips, came to the gate and went out onto the sidewalk. On my way, I started to relax a little. The early summer sun was warm, and the neighborhood smelled of fresh-mown grass and sweet lilacs.

Strolling down the sidewalk, I checked off landmarks in my head. There was the big juniper hedge after Mrs. Baker's yard—aromatic, but prickly! Then a gravel driveway and a chain-link fence. After that, I reached to my left for the mailbox and street sign pole at the corner.

I knew this was a four-way intersection, so I listened

for traffic to stop at the corner. I waited to make sure there weren't any cars coming from the other direction.

All clear! But as I stepped off the curb a sudden hiss of movement surprised me. Before I could step back, something hard slammed into my leg, knocking me to the pavement. I heard myself scream as the fender and handlebars of a bike landed on top of me and pinned my leg against the curb.

Later, waiting for the X-rays of my leg and ankle, Aunt Rose let me have it. "For the 10 days left of your visit, you will leave the house with only me. Do you understand? I care about you too much to allow something like this to happen again!"

"But, Aunt Rose . . . " I tried to tell her I could do it, that I *had* to do things for myself. She wouldn't listen. Driving home, I felt like I was wrapped up as tightly as the doctor had done my ankle.

The next morning I was awake with the birds. I'd thought of a new plan! Aunt Rose had a hair appointment in the morning, so I would have a couple of hours to work. I could hardly keep myself from chuckling as I promised Aunt Rose I'd stay out of trouble. Everything was working out perfectly!

When she drove away I headed for the kitchen, eager to get started. "Francis," I said loudly, "if you're in here you'd better move out of my way. I've got a birthday cake to bake!"

I had a recipe already in mind—one I'd made lots of

times before. First, I turned on the oven. It was like the one I used at home, so I knew to turn it clockwise to the first setting—BAKE. Next, I turned the temperature dial clockwise as far as it would go, then back again until it was just halfway around from OFF. That made it about 350 degrees. I opened the oven and made sure the racks were right where I wanted them. I also felt to make sure heat was coming from the bottom element instead of the top. I didn't want to broil the birthday cake!

The ingredients were easy to find. Flour and sugar were in canisters on the counter. After a little exploring in the cupboard, I found the small, round container of baking powder and the tall, thin bottle of vanilla. Eggs, milk and margarine were in the refrigerator, of course. Once, at home, I confused a carton of orange juice with a carton of milk, so I was careful to check this, too.

I found a big mixing bowl, measuring cups—those are easy to recognize—and the rectangular cake pan. Now I was ready to mix! Measuring wasn't too diffi-cult. I leveled the ingredients in the cup with my fin-gers and brushed the extra into the sink. My father always calls me a "natural chef" because I get my fin-gers and hands into everything when I'm baking. As long as the hands are clean, why not?

When everything was mixed I poured the batter into the pan, tapping and feeling to make sure it was level. As I put the cake in the oven, my sore ankle started to bother me, so I was glad to rest awhile. "Now we just have to wait, Francis," I said. The big cat rubbed against my good leg.

Two hours later, Aunt Rose walked through the door. I was just putting the finishing touches on the frosting. "Stay in there and close your eyes," I called.

"Happy birthday to you . . . ," I sang, making my grand entrance with the cake and trying hard not to limp. Luckily, Francis was not in the doorway. I put the cake on the table, next to the big bouquet of flowers from the garden. "Okay, you can open your eyes now!"

"What a beautiful cake! Did you do this by yourself?"

"Yep. And the dishes are washed; the kitchen is neat. I didn't even burn down the house! Not bad for a blind girl, huh?"

"Not bad at all. You amaze me, you know that? I don't know how I missed it before, but you are a very capable young woman." She gave me a big hug, and I started to feel good again.

"I just wish we had some ice cream to go with it," I commented wistfully.

"Why don't *you* walk to the store and get some, while I clean up. I'll invite some friends over and we'll make it a real party!"

I couldn't believe my ears. I practically flew out the door. The next 10 days weren't going to be so bad after all!

The Halloween That Stunk

*I didn't want any part of Hummer's plan,
but there was never a good time to say no.*

by Sigmund Brouwer

THE HALLOWEEN THAT STUNK

Here's advice you can have for free. Leave dead skunks where they belong. On the side of the road. It was advice I repeated to Hummer.

"Give me a break," she said, jabbing my chest with her forefinger to emphasize each word. She does that as much as possible to prove she can be as tough as any guy. "This is October 31. Remember? Halloween."

"It's also dark," I pointed out unnecessarily. If the dead skunk heaped on the ground beside us didn't smell so bad, we never would have found it on our return. A country road like this has no lights. Lots of strange rustlings in the trees along the road, but no lights.

"It's also cold," I continued above the wind and what I hoped was only the rustling of dry leaves. "No matter *what* day it is, dead skunks don't make me happy."

I didn't point out that I was also scared of what she had planned. It's not smart to let Hummer know she's actually *twice* as tough as any guy.

"Why not?" she challenged. "Scared?"

Hummer and her mom have been my next-door neighbors for as long as I can remember. Which means by now she can read my mind.

"Well, I'd rather be in a pirate's costume getting bagfuls of candy."

Hummer snorted. "Samuel, don't you think 12's a little old for that kind of begging?" She paused, then imitated the kids we'd heard going door to door on our way out of town. "Trick or treat! Trick or treat!" Then she spit. "Bah. Treats just rot your teeth. But tricks, those are too cool."

Hummer is not only tough, but stubborn and determined to do whatever she pleases, whether people like it or not. Trying to stop her is like trying to stop a thunderstorm.

I think Hummer wants to prove to the whole world that nothing matters to her. Nothing. Not even that her dad ran away when she was a baby. Or that everybody knows about the envelope with no return address that her mother gets once a week with cash inside from someone in town—some mystery person who understands how badly they've always needed money.

I can't prove my theory, though. I only asked once, and in reply, Hummer caught me with a punch so fast even she didn't know it would happen. She cried and apologized while I bled from my nose and apologized, and neither of us ever mentioned her dad or the money gifts again.

She hummed now as I fumbled to get my flashlight from my knapsack. "Too cool," Hummer repeated softly between tunes. "A dead-skunk trick is too cool."

What could I say? Especially since too much of this had been my idea. Of course, at the time—barely four hours ago—I'd just been joking.

Hummer and I had been in the backseat of the car, returning from a visit to see my grandmother who lives a few miles out of town. Mom was behind the wheel, gritting her teeth at every car that passed, when all of us groaned at the stench that suddenly filled our nostrils.

"Could you speed up just a little, Mrs. Leslie?" Hummer gagged and pleaded. "That skunk must have sprayed the entire county before it died."

"It was someone going too fast who killed that poor creature in the first place," Mom said. "And I never take chances with my baby in the front."

On cue, my 6-month-old little brother had woken up and started to howl. Under cover of that noise, I had whispered to Hummer, "No wonder he's crying. Imagine waking up to a smell like that."

Hummer had stopped holding her nose to stare at me in thought. Then she had grinned. "Imagine that," she said. "Just imagine that."

So now it was two hours after supper, and we were back at the same spot three miles from the edge of town. Hummer was equipped with rubber gloves, and I had a big plastic bag. We were ready to disregard my advice about leaving dead skunks where they belonged.

The only thing making me feel better was that Hummer lost the coin toss and had to be the one to carry the skunk back to town.

"Samuel, for the last time," she said, "this is foolproof. Didn't your mom mention that Old Lady Lutz won't be back until tomorrow afternoon?" Hummer hummed some more—which is why she had that nickname. Whenever she was impatient (almost always) she hummed. Just like some people strum their fingers or tap their feet.

Foolproof or not, I didn't like this. In fact, I knew it was wrong. But it was like being on the ridge of a slippery roof. One wrong step puts you on the slope; then all of a sudden you're sliding out of control and about to fall off the edge of the roof.

Same with this. You make a half-joke about something, and then you laugh when Hummer takes it further with a plan that sounds funny. You work it out just in theory, and suddenly it seems there never was a good time to say no. So there you are in front of Old Lady Lutz's house, waiting for her neighbors' lights to go off in the house across the street so you can deliver a dead skunk.

I voiced those doubts aloud.

"Foolproof or not, this might be too much," I whispered.

"To an old skinflint like her?"

"Well—"

Hummer began jabbing her finger in my chest again. "Besides, doesn't your dad crack up like crazy when he tells you about some of the Halloween stunts his uncles pulled when they were growing up?"

In the moonlight, her short, blonde hair looked silver.

I pushed her finger aside. "Well—"

"How about when they moved your great-granddad's

outhouse back a few feet?" she asked. "And when he walked up to it in the middle of the night, he—"

"Fine, fine," I said quickly. "Let's just get this over with."

And at that moment, the front hall light across the street went out. The rest of the lights followed, and within moments, the shadows around us were deep enough for action.

Hummer stopped humming.

"Now's the time, bud!"

She grabbed my arm and dragged me to Old Lady Lutz's mailbox, stuck on a post at the edge of the street where the mailman could reach it easily.

She looked quickly in both directions.

"Samuel, open it!"

I sighed. And opened it.

She pulled the plastic bag from her knapsack and pushed it inside, then peeled the plastic back from the dead skunk. It was difficult not to gag at the stench.

"Done!" she said. She carefully folded the plastic, placing that and her rubber gloves inside another plastic bag.

I noticed the little red flag pointing up on the mailbox, telling the mailman there were letters waiting to be posted.

"Hummer, there was mail in there."

Hummer shrugged. "Then Happy Halloween for the mailman, too."

It was the talk of the school for two days. How the mailman—who had a bad cold and couldn't smell a thing—had reached in and grabbed the letters and the skunk at the same time. How after she got home, Old Lady Lutz had calmly chopped the mailbox down and burned it among her raked fall leaves. How nobody could figure out who had played such a cool Halloween trick.

After school on the second day, I stopped by Hummer's house. She was in the kitchen.

"Hummer," I shouted. "What's this! You *never* bake cookies."

"I do now," she said.

"Not too well," I told her. Pans and dough and spoons were everywhere across the counter and sink.

She smiled sadly. "I'll get better as I do it more."

That's when I noticed the tears in her eyes.

"Hummer—" I began as I sat down at the kitchen table.

"Don't," she warned me. "Don't even ask."

I didn't. Instead, I gradually noticed a smell. *Skunk.*

"Hummer?"

"I said not to ask."

Then I looked closely at the small pile of mail on the table in front of me. One of the envelopes had no return address, and through its ripped corner, I could see the edges of some $10 bills.

Hummer had her back to me as she reached for a

container of sugar. I pulled the envelope free and brought it close to my face.

My eyes watered. *Skunk.*

Then I understood. *Through the rain or snow . . .*

The mailman had delivered that batch of letters tucked in the mailbox beside the dead skunk.

"I hope Old Lady Lutz likes your cookies," I told Hummer.

And now that I think of it, Hummer never did jab me or anyone else in the chest again.

Mightier Than Jungle Magic

*For once, the witchdoctor faced
a greater power.*

by Marie Sontag

MIGHTIER THAN JUNGLE MAGIC

Katie looked out the window of the twin-engine Cessna and stared at the jungle below. The missionary pilot, Bob Wilson, nudged Katie's dad and shouted, "That's the valley where your friends, the Arnetts, live. Hang on! Our landing may be a little rough." Bob pushed forward on the controls and began his descent.

Katie gave her mom a worried look.

Brushing aside Katie's long black hair, she asked, "Are you okay, honey?"

Katie nodded, but her whitened face betrayed her anxiety.

Flying close to the ground, they circled a village near the river.

"Do the Arnetts work in that village?" Katie's dad asked.

"No. They work with the Dyaks on the east side of the Suka River," Bob shouted. "That's an Iban village. They aren't nearly as friendly as the Dyaks! Hold on now. Here's our landing strip."

Katie's dark eyes widened as she looked out the window again. Below was a crude clearing of rocks and mud. The landing gear touched the ground, jostling everyone back and forth. Katie feared she would lose her lunch. Finally the plane jerked to a halt.

Bob turned and smiled. "Welcome to Kalimantan!"

Next morning the Arnetts' 16-year-old son, Nick, offered Katie a canoe ride down the Suka River. "Is it safe?" Katie asked her dad.

"Nick has grown up in this country," he replied. "I'm

sure you'll be fine."

Twenty minutes later, Katie and Nick were paddling down the Suka. Katie scooped up a handful of water and splashed her face. "So what's it like being a missionary kid? Do you ever get used to this muggy weather?"

Nick laughed. "After a while it's not so bad. The hardest part is going to Singapore for high school. At least I get to spend my summers with Mom and Dad." Nick paddled on the left and then on the right. "What grade are you going into this fall?"

"Seventh. I wanted to stay home this summer, but—"

"Shhh." Nick pressed a finger to his lips. "Get your camera ready. There's an orangutan up ahead."

Katie grabbed her Nikon and clicked several pictures. "It's huge!" she exclaimed. "What other animals are on this island?"

"If we're lucky, maybe we'll see a crocodile or a python!" Nick flashed a teasing smile.

"May-maybe we should go back now," Katie stuttered.

"We'll be fine as long as we're in the dugout." Nick's strong, tanned arms propelled the canoe farther down the river. Katie framed his firm, round race and brown curly hair in her camera's viewfinder. *I can't wait to show my friends how I spent my summer,* Katie thought as she clicked again.

Nick steered the canoe closer to shore. "I think I see

someone up in that tree." He pointed off to the right.

Suddenly a loud crash made Katie drop her camera. "What was that?"

Through the trees they saw a dark-skinned boy, about 10 years old, pick himself up off the ground and limp into the forest. "He was watching us from that tree until his branch broke," Nick observed, rowing closer. Then he spotted a rope ladder hanging down the river-bank into the water.

Katie saw the rope, too, and shook her head. "You don't plan on getting out here, do you?"

"That boy may have hurt himself. I want to make sure he's okay."

Katie reluctantly followed Nick up the rope ladder.

"Are we still in friendly Dyak territory?" she asked as they tromped through the jungle undergrowth.

"Actually, I think that rope ladder belongs to a group of Ibans," Nick admitted. "But when their ladder hangs all the way down into the water, it means visitors are welcome."

"Oh, now that *really* makes me feel a lot safer." Katie shook her head.

Soon Nick spotted the boy sitting on the ground. He tried to get up and run away, but fell again. Nick spoke to him and then translated for Katie. "I told him not to be afraid," Nick explained. He examined the boy's ankle. "It looks broken. We'd better take him to his village." Nick stooped and picked the boy up.

The boy gave Nick a worried look. "You are one of the white missionaries who live with the Dyaks, aren't you?"

"That's right. My name is Nick."

"I am Ingan. Sometimes I sneak away to listen to the white woman's stories when she teaches the Dyak children—stories about the man Jesus. But please, put me down before you reach my village. It is not safe for you there."

"But your ladder touched the water." Nick looked puzzled.

"I was sent to pull the ladder up," Ingan explained. "Indonesian soldiers set up outposts near our old village, so we moved here. Now the soldiers have come here also. The witchdoctor says it is time to make war."

Suddenly several men wielding spears jumped out of the bushes. "Aiee!" they shouted, surrounding Katie and Nick.

A man wearing bracelets made of animal teeth took Ingan into his own arms. He then shouted orders to the other men. The Iban warriors pointed their spear tips at Katie and Nick, nudging them forward.

"What's going on?" Katie cried.

"He's talking so fast!" Nick tried to calm himself. He listened again as they were pushed along. "The guy giving orders is a witchdoctor. He says the gods told him to capture all foreigners." Nick's voice sounded tight.

When they reached the village, the natives bound Katie's and Nick's hands and pushed them down next to a group of captured Indonesian soldiers. Iban villagers sat in a large circle surrounding the prisoners.

The witchdoctor pulled out a large knife. Katie noticed a piece of long black hair attached to the knife's handle. The witchdoctor closed his eyes and began to chant.

"What's he going to do?" Katie's voiced cracked. She imagined the witchdoctor adding her own black hair to the knife's handle.

"He's asking the gods to enter h-his body," Nick stuttered. "That knife he's h-holding is the ancient mandau used in the Ibans' head-hunting days."

The witchdoctor pointed his knife at the Indonesian soldiers. "The foreigners will no longer push us off our land," he shouted. "We will line our homes with their heads!"

He waved the knife above his own head. "The gods have also told us to rid ourselves of the white people." The witchdoctor pressed the knife to Nick's throat.

"No!" Ingan cried. "The whites have done nothing to hurt us. I have seen their medicines heal those whom you say cannot be healed."

"How dare you speak against me!" the witchdoctor screamed. Turning to Ingan, he yanked a bone off a string around his neck and, cradling the bone in his hand, began to chant.

"We've got to pray hard," Nick whispered to Katie. "I've seen witchdoctors supernaturally kill people when they chant over bones like that."

A chill ran down Katie's spine. She and Nick prayed.

"Your bone has no power over me," Ingan declared. "The gods you invite to come inside of you are evil. I have learned of Jesus Christ, the only true God, and have invited Him to live inside of me. He will defeat your magic."

At those words, the witchdoctor fell to the ground as though dead. Stunned into silence, everyone stared at the prone figure while a group of soldiers rushed into the clearing. They were followed by Nick's and Katie's parents.

The soldiers freed the prisoners. Mr. Arnett checked the witchdoctor's pulse. "He's still alive," he reported.

"It looks like Ingan is the hero of the day!" Nick exclaimed as he walked over to him.

Ingan smiled up at Nick. "No. Jesus is the hero today. I think our people are ready to hear more about Him now."

The Raid on Rebellair

Can you rescue your friend from this stronghold of evil?

by Ray Seldomridge

The year is 1192. Your friend Katherine is being held prisoner in the wicked castle of Rebellair. You can think of nothing but her rescue.

Under dark clouds, you approach the fortress disguised as a peddler. The drawbridge spans a foul-smelling moat. Halfway across it, you hear a guard shout something like "Stay! Who goes there?" Do you stop and wait for the guard to examine you? *Go to 4.* Instead, do you break into a run and try to bypass the guard into the castle? *Go to 10.* Or do you panic and dive into the moat? *Go to 18.*

1 The air is clammy in this dim, musty chamber. At one end is a table draped in scarlet, and a wooden cross lies discarded on the floor. You realize this is the chapel. But cobwebs cover everything; no one has used this room for a long time. Leaving, you ascend a narrow staircase. If you try the door on the second landing, *go to 5.* If you proceed farther up the stairs, *go to 16.*

2 With one glance around, it becomes obvious that you've reached the pantry. Baked breads and other foodstuffs fill the shelves that line the room. Two servants playing chess on top of a crate look up guiltily as you enter. You decide to trust them and ask the whereabouts of the prisoner. They know nothing, but they *did* hear some screaming a week ago when a stranger was brought to the castle. Two small staircases descend from the pantry. If you try the left, *go to 14.* If you pick

the right, *go to 17.*

3 "Now look at you," whispers a kitchen maid who is drawing water from a well. "May I fetch you a drink?" You accept her kind offer. Amidst the honking of geese at her feet, she adds, "Just do not tell anyone. The lord of this place forbids sharing with strangers." You ask if she knows where a prisoner is being held. She suggests you try someone of higher status who might know. If you decide to approach a young page (son of a nobleman), *go to 13.* If you climb the outer stairs to survey the courtyard, *go to 15.*

4 "Peace, friend!" you call. "I sell small knifes and cooking tools. May I speak to the steward?" The soldier denies your request but offers to take you to the baker. Following him across the bailey (courtyard), you enter a small, dark corridor in the foreboding tower known as the keep. The soldier begins to ascend a spiral staircase. If you stay with him, *go to 11.* If you break away and hurtle *down* the stairs, *go to 18.*

5 You have stumbled into the garrison. Several soldiers in full armor are talking in front of the rows of straw beds. "Well, well," says one turning to you. "Are ye lost?" Thinking quickly, you tell him you were sent to bring water to the prisoner. He replies, "Fool! The dungeon is below. Now be gone!" Not trusting him, you decide to proceed *up* the staircase instead. *Go to 16.*

6 Quickly you slide or rappel down the side of the keep. When you finally reach the ground, you duck into the nearest shed, which turns out to be a wood-working shop. "Good carpenter!" you gasp breathlessly. "Grant me a place to hide from evil men!"

"There is only one Good Carpenter," he says with a smile. "And He lived in Nazareth. But haste, I have no hiding place here. Do try the granary next door." You find the granary door locked, so you climb on top and throw yourself through a hole in the roof. *Go to 9.*

7 In the smoky torchlight, you see several dozen men lounging at tables. The evil baron himself leans over the head table, drooling and guzzling a large gob-let of wine. No one seems to notice the minstrel play-ing his pipe, or the juggler tossing balls into the air. "A pretty wench, the prisoner is!" roars one of the drunken knights. "What future befalls her, my lord?" Suddenly you make eye contact with the guard from the gate-house. "Imposter!" he cries. If you run up the nearest staircase, *go to 12.* If you try a side door, *go to 1.*

8 Intense heat strikes your face as you enter the build-ing. A sweaty blacksmith or armorer is hammering a shield on an anvil, while his foot pumps a baffle that blows on the fire. Dozens of swords, spears, battle-axes and helmets hang on pegs around the walls. " 'Tis no place for you, my man!" he hollers. You agree with a nod and walk out. If your thirst drives you to the well,

go to 3. Otherwise you try talking to a page (son of a nobleman). *Go to 13*.

9 Ooof! You land safely on a big stack of hay. Then you climb down and crawl behind a giant column of flour sacks in the dark granary. You wait, listening for your pursuers. A groan nearby startles you. Peering around, you spot a figure lying in the corner. You edge closer and see that the person is bound and gagged. Katherine! You remove the gag and cut the ropes. "Bless the King of Kings!" she whispers. "I thought my prayers were for nothing." After she has had time to rub life back into her wrists and ankles, the two of you head for the postern gate. Freedom is near! □

10 A portcullis (iron gate) slams down in front of you, then another behind. Trapped, you scan the walls for an escape route. But sharp arrows are pointed at you through loopholes on either side, and the "murder hole" in the ceiling glows with hot coals about to be dumped on your head. You call out that it's all a mistake; you thought the guard had said, "Yea, you may go here."

Frowning as he does at all peddlers, the guard grudgingly raises the inner portcullis and lets you into the bailey (courtyard). If you head for a wooden building nearby, *go to 8*. If you walk over to the well, *go to 3*.

11 The kitchen is in a flurry. A butcher glazes the head of a roasted pig, while the baker pulls a score of loaves from the oven. Many servants are running to and from the room with trays of food. "Now is not the time to talk," says the baker to you. "My lord's knights are ravenous from their latest thieving and killing. If I don't make haste, I will be their next victim!" In a whisper, you urge him to escape the castle. Then you ask about the girl. He knows of no such prisoner. Do you descend the spiral staircase? *Go to 2.* Or do you grab a tray of food and enter the Great Hall disguised as a servant? *Go to 7.*

12 Hiding around the corner, you peek into the solar—the warm, private chamber of the baron and his lady. Rich gold and purple tapestries cover the walls on either side of the fireplace. The baroness is combing her hair, while a tailor works on a new dress. Other noblewomen sit on the canopied bed, filing their nails and chatting about their priceless jewels. If you head upstairs, *go to 5.* But if you creep downstairs and take a side door to avoid the Great Hall, *go to 1.*

13 The young man wears a thick leather glove on his right hand, and upon it sits a hawk. You wait until a noisy hunting party has passed, then ask the page if he can direct you to the castle jail. "Bah!" he replies. "I would not concern myself with such scum. Here, have you any knowledge of falconry? The sport of gentlemen, it truly is! You see, . . ." You bow quickly and leave him. At wit's end, you gather up courage to head for the keep, the main tower where soldiers are likely to be found guarding the castle's dungeon. You climb the keep's stairs to the kitchen. *Go to 11.*

14 The acrid smell of mold assaults your nose. In the dim light you see rows of wine barrels. A scuttling sound gives away the presence of rats in this cellar. Suddenly out of the shadows emerges the butler. "Good morrow," he says as he passes you. You notice tears glistening on his cheeks and ask him what is wrong. "I serve the Lord Christ with my heart," he replies after a pause, "but I serve this evil baron with my hands. I cannot escape; neither can I bear to go on." You try to encourage him with words of Scripture. Then you either pass through a tiny hatch behind you (*go to 17*) or climb a staircase at the far end (*go to 12*).

15 From the walkway high on the curtain (outer) wall, you look down on the castle courtyard. Scores of serfs are moving about their business, and a dog-and-cat fight has erupted directly below you. But nothing indicates where a prisoner might be held, so you descend and approach the page after all. *Go to 13.*

16 A stiff wind buffets you as you emerge out onto the roof of the keep. Leaning against the battlement, two soldiers are playing "tables" with dice. A flag displaying a red serpent ripples in the breeze. "Stay!" cries one of the soldiers, rising to his feet and grabbing his spear. "Only soldiers are allowed here," growls the other. "You have come to spy on the castle's defenses!" Your denial is lost in the wind, and the soldiers leap at you. If you grab a rope and climb over the edge of the roof, *go to 6*. If you leap off the roof with a faint hope of landing safely below, *go to 9*.

17 Darkness closes in upon you, as does the stench of sewage. You trip over something that sounds like metal chains. Realizing this is the dungeon, you call out for Katherine. No answer. Either she is dead, or she is not here. Groping for a way out, you finally come to a padlocked door. You find a loose stone and use it to smash the lock. Slowly you push the door open and ascend a steep spiral staircase. If you stop at the second flight and open a door, *go to 1*. If you climb two more flights, *go to 5*.

18 Ugh, the water is icy and more putrid than you imagined. Quickly you swim toward the castle, out of the gatehouse's view. You come upon the postern, a small, handleless door in the massive stone wall. You rap on it, but are surprised when it opens. "Alas, I was just leaving," says a man in the costume of a court jester. "A plague on this house and its lord! He finds none of my jokes amusing. Probably has never laughed in his rotten, miserable life!" Wishing to avoid further ridicule from the gatehouse guards, the jester slips through the postern and is gone. You step into the courtyard. If you turn toward the wooden building on your left, *go to 8*. If you decide to speak to a kitchen maid nearby, *go to 3*.

Brenda Bows Out

*How could so much prayer turn into
such a mess?*

by Marianne K. Hering

BRENDA BOWS OUT

I t's surprisingly simple to kidnap your best friend. It all started when I rang the Browns' doorbell. Brenda opened the front door and said, "I'm quitting ballet." She hadn't even changed out of her nightgown. Her arms were folded across her ribs and tucked inside the sleeves of her white bathrobe. It looked like a straightjacket.

"Brenda," I said calmly, preparing for an argument. "Our last rehearsal commences in 10 minutes. The longer you glare at me, the less time you'll have to change clothes."

I was glad I had used the word "commences." It sounded so official. I'd use any ploy to keep her in the group. I'd been praying about it for weeks. This was a crisis I knew God would fix.

"But, Mattie—" she began.

"No 'buts,' " I cut in. "For three years we've slaved away doing *pliés* and *sautés* in every imaginable position. We've only got one more year before we dance in toe shoes—on point."

"But, Mattie—" she tried again.

"Our posture is perfect," I continued. "We walk with our ankles turned out. You can't quit your life's calling."

"Okay, okay," she said. "Wait a second." She closed the door and reappeared in less than five minutes. Pink sweats covered her black leotard, and she carried her slippers in one hand. My speech had worked. I had control. *Thanks, God, for hearing me!* I prayed as we ran to class.

Our instructor most definitely had a "pet." Miss Marissabina Rousseau adored Brenda Brown. That particular Saturday, Miss Rousseau showered admiration all over Brenda's feet.

"Please note, class," she said, "Brenda's perfect point. See the beautiful line? That's created by the heel muscle pulling up. Next year, in toe shoes, I'm sure she'll dance superbly. . . ."

Brenda stood leg and foot extended, drowning in compliments. In a halfhearted effort to even things out, Miss Rousseau began sprinkling blessings on the rest of us.

"My, but you do work hard, Mattie," she said to me later on.

I used the opportunity to tell her that Brenda was dropping ballet class. She blinked her false eyelashes at me and said, "Thank you, Mattie, for informing me."

Miss Rousseau called us girls to gather round. When she had our attention, she asked Brenda to dance in Saturday's performance. "We need you," Miss Rousseau added. Some of the girls snickered. Although Brenda was the best in our class, older ballerinas performed the lead parts. Even Brenda Brown was dispensable.

Brenda was trapped. She didn't want to argue with Miss Rousseau in front of us. "I'll come," she answered.

It was raining by the time our rehearsal ended, so I called my brother Ross and asked him to pick us up. While waiting, Brenda tried to explain.

"I'm not afraid to go on stage," she said. "It's just that Miss Rousseau likes me *too* much. I can't stand listening to her gush over me. It's suffocating. What if Brenda with the perfect feet makes an imperfect *pas de chat?*"

She did have a point, so to speak. I didn't have an answer. But Brenda was our example. If she gave up, what hope was left for the rest of us? Besides, I had been praying.

"Well," I said, choosing my words carefully to sound important, "you're *committed.* If you try and weasel out of the performance, I'll make you go." (Right then, the kidnapping idea formed in my brain.)

And right then, our conversation began to turn into a fight. "I said I'd be there. But after Saturday I'm going to quit dance," she said. "I want to become a candy striper or do more baby-sitting. Anything that isn't so competitive. Dance is too much pressure."

"What a baby!" I squealed. "You're perfect for dance. Everyone says so."

"Well, *I* don't say so," she snapped back. "Dancing is supposed to make you feel free, but it locks me up." We were practically shouting, right there on a public sidewalk.

"You can't be so spineless. You have to keep trying," I demanded. "I've been *praying.*"

"Mattie, you're deaf!" she yelled, then raised her voice even louder. "Now hear this: Saturday is my last day. Then I quit."

I watched my best friend gracefully run off into the rain. I guess she didn't want a ride home.

The night before the performance, I prayed that God would zap some sense into her. But when the phone rang the next morning, I took in some bad news.

I heard Mom say, "Oh, hello, Lorraine (Mrs. Brown), how are you? . . . Oh, no! Brenda can't be sick. Of course I'll have Mattie tell Marissabina. . . . Yes, I can stop and help you at church before going to the performance. We don't need to be at the auditorium early. . . . Mattie? Oh yes, I'm sure she'll understand why Brenda's not showing up. . . ."

Understand? No way. That's when I put my plan into action. I had only two hours to pull it off. So naturally I showered, put on my costume and fixed my hair. One hour gone.

Next I went to find Ross and convince him to join in my mission. (I had to bribe him by promising to do his kitchen chores for a month.)

As we rushed out the door, I saw the note Mom had left. I didn't read it because I knew what it said: No Brenda.

At first, we were going to sneak into the back of Brenda's house, but Ross figured ringing the doorbell was easier. And it was. Brenda's dad worked weekends, and Mrs. Brown was at church with my mom, so Brenda, dressed in robe and nightgown, answered the door.

When she saw Ross, her cheeks flushed, and she

said, "Oh, gosh—my hair's gross."

Then she kind of fainted, from embarrassment or something. Ross gently picked her up and carried her to the car. I never imagined anything so easy.

I ran up the stairs to Brenda's room and grabbed her costume and ballet slippers.

When I got to the car, Brenda wasn't struggling at all. She lay in the back, moaning. Ross had wrapped one seat belt around her knees. Another secured her shoulders and arms. *Piece of cake,* I thought.

"Aww, Mattie," Ross said. "She's really ill. Let her go."

"Don't be silly," I told Ross. I was intent on getting her to the auditorium. "It's just a cold, and we aren't hurting her. Let's just go. One day she'll thank us for this."

Brenda moaned again.

We had about 15 minutes left when we arrived at the auditorium. Ross parked the car and helped me pull Brenda out. Then I half-dragged, half-carried her into the rest room. Somewhere she found her strength, slipped away and locked herself in a stall. She begged over and over, "Please leave me alone."

Needing reinforcement, I ran to find Miss Rousseau. When I told her of Brenda's state, her eyelashes fluttered in shock. Then she charged into the ladies' room. Seconds later, I crept in and handed over Brenda's costume and slippers.

Miss Rousseau had five minutes to talk Brenda into dancing.

Three minutes later they both emerged from the bathroom. Brenda was pale, but in costume.

I lifted up a silent prayer. *Thanks, God. I knew I could make this plan work with Your help.*

Everyone prepared for the big entrance. Once the curtain was up, we twirled and danced. Miss Rousseau had taught us well. I loved it.

The lights blinded me a little, but I could still search the audience. My mom and Mrs. Brown were there. Even Ross had hung around. But not one of them smiled.

I soon saw why: Brenda was stumbling on every move. She did a few weak *glissades* in the wrong direction and spun around. Then she threw up the entire contents of her stomach all over the lead ballerina's satin slippers! Needless to say, the dance did not go on.

Kidnapping just isn't done in our family. Mom grounded me for one week and Ross for two, because he's older. It didn't matter to Mom that no one, not even her own mother, had known Brenda was suffering from the Hong Kong flu.

Being on restriction gave me plenty of time to listen—something new for me. Before then, I hadn't listened to God when I prayed; I'd just told Him what I wanted. And I hadn't listened to Brenda or Ross. I'd done everything my own way, pushing people around.

But now I am motivated. I *have* to listen to God. No one else can help me apologize to Brenda and say that I, Mattie Metzger, am oozing with remorse. That I repent. That I was wrong. That no one ever has to dance again, not one step. (Unless, of course, God decides to change her mind.)

Skunks, Rattlers and Very Good Men

*The new teacher was determined
to make the boys learn.*

by Nancy N. Rue

J osé slipped into the mining shack schoolroom. He noticed that even Matthew Breckenridge had arrived early to get a look at the new teacher. Matthew's father and the mine owners had brought her to Arizona all the way from Connecticut.

"She'll *whip* learning into these boys," Isaac Breckenridge had said at the town meeting, according to rumor.

But it was a wispy girl who stood behind the barrel desk. She was barely as tall as 11-year-old Matthew, and she didn't look strong enough to whip butter. José saw Matthew smirk.

"Good morning, gentlemen," she said in a surprisingly firm voice. The boys mumbled.

"I am Miss Cara. Let us take out our slates."

The boys looked at her blankly. José wasn't sure what a slate was.

"What's the matter?" Miss Cara said.

"We haven't got 'ny slates," Matthew said.

Miss Cara's eyes scanned the room, and the boys nodded.

"You have no ink then either?" she said. "No copy books?"

Just then a shrill sound—four blasts—pierced the air. *It's the mine whistle,* José thought. *But was it really? It had sounded different.*

"Indians!" Matthew cried. "It could be an Apache attack. We have to get into the mine tunnel!"

"Just a minute, gentlemen," Miss Cara said. She passed quietly to the door. José peeked outside. The morning bustle in the mining camp looked normal.

"False alarm," she said.

"But, Miss Cara—"

Her eyes darted to Matthew. "We'll wait for another whistle," she said. "Perhaps one that comes from *outside* this classroom."

Matthew's eyes glinted back at her. He tossed his head.

"In fact, gentlemen," Miss Cara said, "let's walk outside now and use the dirt for slates. You all have fingers, so we'll use them as well."

Moments later, each boy was sitting on the ground, drawing a square in the dirt.

"We will begin with the alphabet," Miss Cara said.

The few who had gone to school in the East before moving to Arizona seemed to know what to do, but the Mexican boys like José just blinked and stared.

Miss Cara smiled. "We will begin with A," she said, pulling out a piece of charred wood that she had found in the schoolroom's stove. "A," she said as she wrote with it on the shack wall. "Now draw."

José made a shaky A in his square. This was exactly why he'd begged his father to let him come to the new school. He was 10 and old enough to work, but he wanted to learn to read and write—even a little.

"Matthew?" Miss Cara said. Matthew was sullenly

117

scuffling at the dirt with his foot.

"Draw with your toe, then," she said. "But draw."

When school was dismissed at lunchtime, José joined the boys under the lone tree behind the shack. Matthew leaned against it, eyes slanted and head tossing.

"We got work to do, men," he said. He sneered toward the shack. "We got a woman who don't know who's really in charge here."

"Who *is?*" said one of the small boys.

Matthew pushed the boy down. "*We* are, fool!" he said. "And I know how to show her."

The boys drew in around him—all but José who listened silently from the edge of the circle. He didn't like the plan Matthew unfolded.

"Tonight," Matthew finished. "Nine o'clock. There's hardly a moon. Carlos—bring the trap."

José went out that night, but only to walk and pray as he always did. His mother had told him when he was small that if he went to God with his hurts, God would give him an easy feeling.

"*Mi Dios,*" José said to Him that night. "Those boys will drive Miss Cara out. Boys like Matthew are too strong for *me* to stop them—"

José looked hopefully at the white sliver moon. But there was no easy feeling.

No one had gone in when José arrived at school the next day. Miss Cara and the boys were holding their hands over their noses.

"It happens all the time, Miss Cara," Matthew was saying. "A skunk'll just crawl under a building and—phew—it takes weeks to get the smell out."

Miss Cara sighed. "Well, it will take at least today. No one can work in that stench, and it's too windy to work out here."

With disappointed eyes, she looked at the knot of hopeful faces. "Go home, gentlemen," she said. She looked at Matthew. "But I will see you all here tomorrow."

They bolted like jackrabbits set free from a trap, the way José wished the skunk had been set free from the trap Matthew had set under the shack.

With a squaring of her slight shoulders, Miss Cara whipped her scarf off, planted it over her face, and headed for the shack.

"You will get sick!" José cried. She looked back, and José dropped his eyes.

"You *do* speak English," she said.

He nodded shyly.

"Then perhaps you can tell me some things," she said. "These boys are determined not to learn, aren't they?"

José didn't answer.

"What they don't know—what's your name?"

"José," he whispered.

"What they don't know, José, is that I am just as determined as they are. They will learn, and—" She nodded fiercely at him, "—they will become *very good* men."

José couldn't imagine Matthew Breckenridge ever being a "very good man," but if anyone could make him one, it would be Miss Cara.

For the next few days, eyes watered and throats burned from coughing, but Miss Cara taught with a neckerchief tied over her face like a bandit, and gradually the smell of the skunk faded. Soon every boy could write his own name and add up money to buy supplies.

But not Matthew. He put a piece of cactus on Miss Cara's seat or made rattlesnake sounds during the spelling lesson.

Miss Cara never scowled, and José could see the other boys' eyes shining when she talked. Even when Matthew's twisted smile hinted that he had still one more scheme, God's easy feeling slipped into José.

One day, Miss Cara held a spelling bee. The race was down to José and another boy, and their teams were piled three deep cheering them on. Miss Cara stood on her barrel desk.

"HAT!!" she shouted over the din.

But José felt a heavy hand on his shoulder. He looked up into Isaac Breckenridge's angry face.

"What is all this racket?" Breckenridge demanded.

"A spelling bee," Miss Cara said calmly. "Would you like to join us?"

His eyes slanted like Matthew's. "This is a school!"

José saw Miss Cara's mouth harden. "I don't wish to discuss this in front of my students," she said.

"*I* wish to discuss it. Tonight—in the mining office." Mr. Breckenridge turned on his heel. Matthew's eyes gleamed triumphantly.

So that was Matthew's final trick—to set his father on Miss Cara. The easy feeling tightened to a hard one inside of José. She might be able to handle Matthew, but no one was a match for Isaac Breckenridge.

José was out telling that to God that night when he heard voices.

"There's no learning going on. It's nothing but a barnyard full of wild animals—"

Mr. Breckenridge.

"You have no idea what those boys—"

Miss Cara.

They were silhouetted in the window of the mining office. José crouched down.

Mr. Breckenridge said, "We brought you here to make these boys behave in school. In Tombstone, the schoolmaster raises his boys by the hair and bangs their heads—"

"Why on *earth?*"

"That's what it takes," he said.

"No," Miss Cara said. "I cannot believe their parents would want that," Miss Cara said.

"We'll see! Tomorrow night we'll hold a town meeting and vote. Be here."

The door slammed, and José tightened into a ball. When the footsteps had faded, he searched the sky.

"*Mi Dios,*" he whispered. "Please help."

The room smelled of a rotting animal the next morning. A final insult from Matthew, José knew. But Miss Cara pulled the dead squirrel out of her barrel desk and commanded the boys to follow her outside. She sat them by the tree and read. Only Matthew stalked away. *He's acting like she's gone already,* José thought.

But his thoughts were split by a scream.

"Help me!" someone cried.

It was Matthew, face to face with a rattlesnake.

"No one move," Miss Cara said. "Matthew—don't move."

As the boys watched like statues, Miss Cara picked up a rock and walked steadily to where the snake thrust its tongue at Matthew.

No! José wanted to cry. Let *Matthew* be struck, Miss Cara. Not you!

But just as the snake pulled back its arrow-shaped head, she slammed the rock down with both hands—

again and again—until the snake's remains lay still at Matthew's feet.

José felt sick. Miss Cara let the rock drop.

"Are you all right?" she said.

Matthew's face cracked like an eggshell, and he sobbed in raspy gasps.

"Cry," Miss Cara said. "Anyone would do the same."

Matthew nodded dumbly and continued to sob.

"But let me tell you this," she went on. "This would not have happened if you had been where you were supposed to be. Now you are welcome to join us."

She marched back to the boys. They watched Matthew smear his wet face with his sleeve and slowly walk toward them.

It was dark when José saw the shadowy forms going to the mining hall.

Heads turned when he reached the doorway. He looked around wildly and almost ran, but his eyes found Miss Cara, sitting on the edge of the circle of townspeople.

"What do you want, boy?" Isaac Breckenridge boomed.

"I . . . I came to speak for Miss Cara," a bird-like voice quavered. José froze. It was *his* voice, and he was scared. But then he caught Miss Cara's smile. Her eyes said, *I've taught you to be a very good man.* "We . . . we want—" José stammered.

SKUNKS, RATTLERS AND VERY GOOD MEN

Another voice suddenly rose at José's back. "What he's meanin' to tell you, sir"—it was Matthew—"is that we want her to stay."

Talent Night

Stefan and his violin were in a tight squeak.

by John F. Hudson

TALENT NIGHT

Mrs. Pompano bustled down the church hallway, the bulletin boards fluttering as she passed. "Now there is just the one I wanted to see!" she huffed. She cornered Stefan and his mother by the sanctuary door.

"I hear Stefan is a fine violinist. You will play for the Annual Family Talent Night, won't you, Stefan?"

Stefan began to shrink.

"Of course he'll play," Stefan's mother answered. "He learned a very nice piece just last month, didn't you, Stefan?" She reached down to take Stefan by the shoulder and discovered his cap instead. "For goodness sake, Stefan, stand up!"

"My violin squeaks," Stefan said.

"Well, you can oil it or whatever you do with squeaky violins," his mother said. "Your sister can accompany you on the piano so nobody will hear the squeaks."

"Yes, they will," he said.

"You play very well after only one year of lessons. You should be glad to show everyone what you can do!"

"Brahms' 'Lullaby'?"

"That's a beautiful piece."

Stefan sighed and shrank again.

Stefan's mother brought her famous lamb-and-egg-plant casserole to the Talent Night dinner. Stefan's sister, Sophia, heaped her plate up twice. She was 16 and had been playing the piano forever. Nothing bothered her. Stefan didn't eat. His stomach had squeezed down to the size of a walnut.

At 7 o'clock Mrs. Pompano stood up, and everyone around her began to clang spoons against glasses and coffee cups. "Time to begin," she said. "Our first talented performers this evening are Viola and Constance Macey. They are going to sing for us two of the songs they did last month for the Red Cross benefit."

The Macey sisters were as old as Stefan's mother. They sang every year. Everyone thought they should join the opera in New York. Stefan slid down in his seat.

Next came Chloe Perkins. She played first violin for the Caminstown orchestra. "Here's a piece I know you'll like," she said. " 'The Flight of the Bumblebee.' "

The room hushed. Miss Perkins stood tall, with her violin pointed straight out from her neck and her bow arm lifted. Then the "bumblebee" dove and zoomed as her fingers moved in a blur on the strings. The room stood up to applaud. Stefan looked at his sister. She was still eating a piece of chocolate cake.

"Now, let's have something a little different," Mrs. Pompano said. "Marla Jones is one of our high school cheerleaders, and she is going to show us how to twirl the baton."

Marla bounced up in her short, pleated cheerleader's skirt and switched on a cassette player. When the music began, she spun her baton from hand to hand and over her head and around her back. Then as the march drew

127

near the end she tossed her baton toward the ceiling.

As it came whirling down, she reached and missed. The baton clattered on the floor. Stefan looked around. Everyone was waiting. Marla picked up her baton and tossed it again high in the air. This time she caught it, and everyone cheered. Stefan sat up a little straighter.

Then Linda Malley, who was in the fifth grade with Stefan, played the piano. Stefan heard a number of mistakes, but still everyone applauded. They were having a good time.

The Carson family came next. Harry Carson began with a long explanation of how he had always admired families who did things together; so last Christmas when he saw some recorders—long, wooden instruments that looked like clarinets and played like whistles—he bought four of them, enough for his whole family.

"We're going to show you what we have learned," he said. After three false starts, they managed to get through "Mary Had a Little Lamb" and "Twinkle, Twinkle, Little Star." Again everyone applauded.

"I think it's wonderful," Stefan's mother said, "the way their whole family gets together like that to make music."

"What music?" Stefan whispered.

"Shhh!" said his mother.

It was beginning to look as if Brahms' 'Lullaby' might survive a few squeaks.

Now it was Mr. Fuddler's turn. Stefan was next.

"I'm going to play on my Christmas present, too," Mr. Fuddler said, holding up a tiny object. "My daughter gave it to me. It's a nose flute. See? You hold it up here and blow through your nose. I'll try to play 'Pop Goes the Weasel' without sneezing. Here goes!"

Everybody ducked. Laughter was bouncing off the walls by the time he finished.

It took several minutes for Mrs. Pompano to collect herself. "Here is our newest talent," she said finally. "Stefan Stamas accompanied by his sister, Sophia. Stefan is going to play Brahms' 'Lullaby.' "

Stefan picked up his violin to follow Sophia to the piano. "See if there's any cake left," he whispered to his mother. "I'm hungry."

Brave As a Lion

A story about the man who changed medicine forever.

by Susan C. Hall

BRAVE AS A LION

Back in 1865, surgeons knew little about germs or the causes of infection. So wounds and surgical instruments were not cleaned before an operation. When Dr. Joseph Lister of Scotland began doing it, everyone just laughed. . . .

As dawn broke, 11-year-old Jaimie Greenless stumbled out his front door. He rubbed his bleary eyes and began his long walk to work. The streets were filled with others on their way to the shipyards or to one of the many factories in Glasgow.

Suddenly, Jaimie spotted a finely dressed man and woman walking just ahead of him.

What are they doing here in the slums? he wondered. He darted through the crowd and fell into step behind the fancy couple.

"Oh, Joseph," Jaimie heard the woman say, "my heart aches for these slum people. Why must they live in such squalor?"

"Industry is b-b-booming in Glasgow," said the man, stuttering slightly. "People are flocking here by the h-hundreds, looking for work. When there are too many workers, wages are low."

"Joseph, doesn't it seem odd that the university would be located right in the middle of these slums? Maybe your appointment here is a sign that God wants you to take care of these people."

"P-Perhaps you're right, Agnes," said the man. "I'm

told working conditions are dangerous, causing many accidents."

Jaimie knew this was true. Last week, James Wylie, a friend and fellow factory worker, had caught his arm between a pulley and a belt. His forearm was broken, and the skin torn open. Everyone said the doctors would surely amputate the arm.

Jaimie shuddered now as he thought about it.

The man and woman paused, then turned and walked up the steps of a red brick building that Jaimie knew was the university hospital. He watched them go inside.

At that moment, he realized he'd been dawdling. Not looking where he was going, he dashed into the street. Suddenly he felt a horse-drawn cart hit him; everything went black.

When Jaimie came to, he found himself lying on the table. His left leg throbbed, and he was terrified.

A man approached him. "Hello, J-J-Jaimie. I'm Dr. Lister."

"I saw you earlier," said Jaimie. "Walking along the street with a lady."

Dr. Lister smiled. "Yes, that was my wife, Agnes. She frequently accompanies me to w-w-work to h-help me with my research."

"Am I in the hospital?" asked Jaimie.

Dr. Lister nodded. "In surgery. You have broken your leg, and the bone has torn through the skin. I'm going to put you to sleep with chloroform. Then I'll operate."

"Don't amputate!" cried Jaimie, thinking of his friend. "No, no, no. Please, Dr. Lister. No."

"I don't believe that will be necessary, Jaimie. You see, I have a plan. First I'll set your leg in a splint. Then I'll cleanse the wound and kill the microbes with carbolic acid. Next, I'll cover it with bandages soaked in the same chemical. I believe this will prevent infection."

Jaimie began to cry. "But what if it doesn't work?"

"It will," said Dr. Lister. "I believe that with the help of our Lord, my idea will succeed." He tousled Jaimie's hair. "Say your prayers, Jaimie boy, and you won't be so frightened. In fact, I'll bet you'll feel brave as a lion."

Jaimie smelled the chloroform only briefly; then once again everything went black.

Waking from the anesthesia was the strangest experience he'd ever had. His eyelids seemed too heavy to lift. He could hear voices, but he couldn't see who spoke.

"What's that strange smell?" asked one voice.

"Carbolic acid," said a second voice. "Dr. Lister has soaked the bandages with it. He thinks this will stop infection."

"I've heard the other doctors talking about Dr. Lister's wild ideas," said the first voice. "They think he's crazy."

"He is," said the second voice. "But you and I are

just lowly medical students. We can only follow orders, even if they're foolish. Mark my words. That leg will have to be amputated."

Panic seized Jaimie.

Dr. Lister lied to me, he thought. But before he could think anymore, he drifted back to sleep.

When Jaimie awoke again, he could open his eyes. He found the doctor standing by his bed.

"You told me a fib, Dr. Lister," cried Jaimie. "You are going to take off my leg."

"You're wr-wr-wrong, Jaimie," said the doctor. "The medical students r-r-report that you have no fever. This is excellent news, because fever is one of the first signs of infection."

"You mean I'll be all right?"

"Yes, I believe you'll be fine. Try to rest now. And don't forget those prayers."

Time passed slowly for Jaimie. His parents visited infrequently, because his father also worked long hours in a factory. His mama had his five younger brothers and sisters to care for. So the lonely, worried boy waited and prayed.

On the fourth day, Dr. Lister arrived to find Jaimie in tears.

"It hurts, Dr. Lister. It hurts worse than ever." Jaimie saw the doctor's face turn pale. "The acid isn't going to work, is it?"

"W-W-We'd b-b-b-better h-have a l-l-l-look," said Dr. Lister. "I'm going to re-re-remove the b-bandages."

He's stuttering more, thought Jaimie. *That means he's worried.* More tears streamed down Jaimie's cheeks.

"R-R-Remember, Jaimie boy. You're as b-b-b-brave as a lion," said Dr. Lister. Then Jaimie saw a smile spread across the doctor's face.

"No wonder you have pain, Jaimie. The carbolic acid has burned your skin. I'll have to dilute the solution. But no real harm has been d-d-done. The important thing is there's no trace of infection. Our prayers have been answered."

Soon staff doctors and medical students crowded around Jaimie's bed.

"Amazing," said one doctor as he looked at Jaimie's leg. "I see none of the usual scarlet-colored inflammation. Quite remarkable."

"God's miracle," said another doctor.

"God's miracle?" asked still another. "My dear doctor, don't you realize that the Almighty has no place in medical science?"

"I disagree," said Dr. Lister. "I have no hesitation in saying th-th-that in my opinion there is no antagonism between the religion of Jesus Christ and any f-fact scientifically established."

Even though some of Dr. Lister's words were unfamiliar, Jaimie understood.

My leg is not infected, thanks to Dr. Lister, he thought. *But the idea wouldn't have succeeded without our faith in God.*

Six weeks and two days after his accident, Jaimie Greenless was discharged from the hospital with two whole legs. Walking down the streets of Glasgow again, he always watched out for horse-drawn carts—and remembered the doctor with the brave new idea.

Ten Miles to the Amen

Jessie wasn't really supposed to talk to strangers.

by Steven J. Sweeney

Please. help.

J essie was first to see the handwritten note. At the last highway rest area before their vacation trip would end, her folks had decided to stop for a must-go picnic lunch. "Everything in that cooler must go," insisted her mother. And her father wanted to check the engine— *again.*

The note, asking for money, was thumbtacked near a state map display in the visitors' center. A plastic mileage tape hung from a circle around a point that said, "You Are Here." Jessie stretched the tape out in all directions. "Here" was in the middle of nowhere. And "Here" was hot.

Jessie's mother spread an old, flower-patterned sheet on the brown August grass and began to poke around in the cooler for a leftovers lunch.

"Mama," called Jessie, half skipping over to the picnic. Dusty looking grasshoppers flew up alongside her. "Some people don't have enough money to get home."

Her mother peered into the cooler.

"What?" she asked, lifting out a package of bologna. She sniffed it, made a face, set the package aside and reached back into the cooler. "What are you talking about, Jessie?"

Jessie handed her the note at the same time that she spotted a vending machine.

"Mama, can I get a Snickers?"

"You'll be lucky if you don't turn into a Snickers after this trip," her mother answered as she began to read the note. "Have an orange instead." Still reading, she held one out in Jessie's direction.

Gross, thought Jessie. *Like I've just been dying for an orange.* "I'd rather turn into a Snickers," she protested. But her mother wasn't listening. Jessie took the orange.

"John," her mother called to Jessie's father, who was jiggling wires on the car engine. Seemed like he was always fussing with the car or the boat or something like that. Jessie's mom said he spent more time talking to his machines than to people. "Come look at this."

Squeals and laughter came from a cluster of birch trees at the other side of the picnic area. Three kids were tearing around, tagging each other and racing away. A boy, one hand clutching the paw of a yellow stuffed bear, just watched. Jessie wandered over, along the edge of the grass.

"Hi," called out the taller girl. "I'm Megan. Want to play?"

Jessie wasn't really supposed to talk to strangers, but before she could answer anyway, the girl asked, "Whatcha got?"

Jessie realized she meant the orange.

"Want some?"

When Jessie handed her a piece, Megan didn't eat it but turned and gave it to the small boy who had appeared beside her with the bear. "That's Michael," she said, indicating with a turn of her head. "He's quiet."

The boy eagerly pushed the whole piece into his mouth, as if he were very hungry. Twice more Megan shared with the others and finally accepted a section for herself.

"Where are your parents?" asked Jessie.

"Over at the truck, in the shade," said Megan, pointing to a rusty blue pickup with a camper shell. "We're kind of out of gas."

"Was that your note in the visitors' center?" asked Jessie.

"Yep," beamed Megan. "Papa said it out loud, and I wrote it. Mama says I'm the best printer in the family."

One of the boys tagged his sister, and they scrambled off again. Jessie watched. She had complained that morning because her cotton pants didn't go with her blouse. But none of these kids' clothes even fit them: tight, or baggy with cuffs rolled up. She studied the truck, then turned and marched back toward her parents. More grasshoppers sprang ahead.

A problem: She had spent all her savings—*12 dollars*—on the trip. But she had an idea, too, that just might work.

"Beth," her father was arguing as Jessie approached. "You can't take everything on faith. We've seen this all over. People just sitting around, waiting for a handout—"

"Daddy," interrupted Jessie, who didn't often interrupt her father. In one breath she said, "Miss Dern at church school says we have to help Jesus by helping others, and I don't think those kids have had anything to eat today." Her father was quiet for a second, so she took another breath and told him her plan.

He didn't like it, of course. Not at all.

"What? Give up your allowance for the next two months? For some people you don't even know? What's gotten into you two?"

But Jessie's mother had set down her pop can and stood up. "Come with us, John," she said, taking Jessie's hand. "It can't hurt to walk over and say hello."

He made a face, waited a few seconds, then got up. With Jessie leading, they approached the truck.

"Howdy," said the man who had been tinkering with what looked like a lawnmower engine, set up on the tailgate of the truck.

Jessie's dad said about as much as usual, she figured. "Um. Saw your note." He pointed with his thumb back over his shoulder. "Troubles?"

"Well," said the man, "yeah." He seemed to have forgotten for a moment why he was parked there. "Left some important parts of the drive shaft on the freeway out of Jefferson yesterday. I was lucky to be able to do the work myself." He tugged on a greasy wrench.

"Mechanic by trade," he explained. "I've been chasing work all over the state, but it runs a pretty good race. Anyway, even used parts ate up most of the gasoline money. Got a deal on this two-cycle from the junk-yard, though. Should be able to resell it. Needed a gas-ket and a new plug is all. Was about to try her out."

He pulled the coiled starter rope. Nothing. He eased a screw one-half turn. Jessie's dad moved in closer, bent low. He watched so intently that his nose wrinkled up under his sunglasses. Another pull, and the engine roared. The man slapped his knee. All the kids held their hands over their ears. Jessie's dad straightened up, folded his arms and grinned.

After the engine was shut down, Jessie's father slipped out his billfold. He didn't seem to quite know what to say. A semi thundered in from the freeway exit and skidded its rear wheels to a stop, releasing an odor of burning rubber into the air.

"What kind of mileage do you get on the pickup?"

"Dad!" moaned Jessie, rolling her eyes. To Megan she explained, "He asks *everybody* that."

Megan's father chuckled. "Truth to tell, we left Three Forks this morning on a tankful of prayers, so I believe we've been pushing along at about ten miles to the Amen."

Jessie's father handed him some money, folded. "Can't hardly beat that, I guess, but maybe you could use some gas, just as a backup."

Jessie poked his leg.

"Oh, and Jessie here wants to chip in for some burgers and fries." He handed over another bill.

"My goodness, thank you, Jessie. God bless you both." He turned and handed the money with both hands to the woman Jessie thought must be Megan's mother. She seemed shy and had said nothing until then, when she smiled slightly and nodded her own thanks.

"Say, didn't you have the hood up yourself a while ago?"

Jessie's father scratched the back of his neck. "Running a little warm. Thermostat, maybe."

"Maybe. Should we take a look?"

So the two of them went over to the car while Jessie's and Megan's moms talked and fanned themselves in the dry heat. Jessie and the others played Red Rover until it was time to leave.

The girls exchanged addresses, promising to write each other. The men latched the car hood and shook hands. Jessie's mom found a few more oranges.

"Good thing we ran into him," said Jessie's father with a new lift in his voice. "He knew right off it wasn't the thermostat after all." He put the car in gear and headed toward the freeway entrance ramp.

"Just waiting for a handout, were you, Dad?" teased Jessie, waving to Megan out the back window. They laughed and couldn't quit until the gray ribbon of freeway had carried them far out of sight.

Think, Nick, Think

*Have you ever wondered what school is like
for a kid who has trouble learning?*

by Pamela Farrel

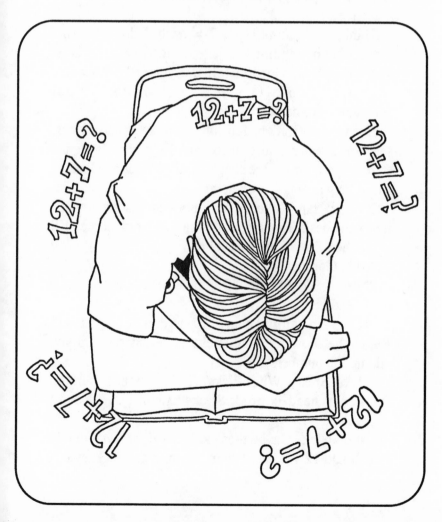

THINK, NICK, THINK

What time is it? I've been working on this math problem forever. My head hurts. I think and think and think, and I still can't figure it out. Hurry, Mrs. Gordon. Maybe you can help me. You're so nice. You make it easier.

Think, Nick, think. 12 + 7 = ? Oh, I don't know. I can't count on my fingers; there are too many numbers. What did Mrs. Gordon tell me yesterday? I can't remember. Think, Nick, think. 12 + 7. It's so hard! Why can't I remember?

Hurry, Mrs. Gordon. Tell Julie to go away and try herself. She's better at math than I am. Help *me*. Maybe if I stare at you, you'll see that I need help. Mrs. Gordon, I'm staring at you. Now help me.

Tap, tap, tap. I like the way my pencil sounds when it hits the desk. Tap, tap, tap. Won't she look at me? I'll yell at her. I'll tell her I need help.

"Mrs. Gordon!"

"Yes, Nick?" She smiled at me when she answered.

"I need help."

"Nick, I'm with Julie now. Try to think of it yourself. Remember how we used sticks yesterday to help you add up the numbers?"

Sticks. Sticks. What sticks? Think, Nick. It hurts to think. My head is tired. Sticks? I can't . . . I can't remember.

Dumb Nick. Maybe those kids are right. I *am* dumb. I can't add 12 + 7, and I'm in the sixth grade! They can all add 12 + 7. Everyone in the whole world can add 12 + 7. I'm so stupid. My head is aching. And my eyes hurt. They are full of hot tears. But I won't let them out. Someone might see them and laugh at me and call me Dumb Baby Nick.

Dumb Nick. That's what they call me at recess. Oh, no! Recess comes after math. I don't want to go outside. I don't want them to call me Dumbo Nick. I just want them to call me Nick, or maybe Nicholas like my mom does.

I wish my mom was here. She knows what 12 + 7 is. She wouldn't call me dumb or fat or stupid. My sisters Jill and Kathy wouldn't either. They would help me.

I want to go outside right now and kick the ball. I can kick the ball hard. I can kick it far. I can kick it past 12 + 7. I can kick it to a place where there isn't any math. I can kick it to a place where they don't call people dumb or fat or stupid. I can kick it way up into the sky where Jesus lives.

Jesus would know what 12 + 7 is. Mom says Jesus knows everything. I wish I knew everything. I wish I just knew what 12 + 7 was. Maybe then people wouldn't call me Dumb Nick or Retarded Nick.

Oh, my head hurts, Jesus. It hurts from all this thinking. 12 + 7 = ? Ugh! Sticks? Hmmm. How can sticks help? How can they help, Jesus? Oh yeah! We drew sticks on my paper and counted with them. I'll draw lots of sticks to make sure I have enough.

| | | | | | | | | | | | | | | | | | | | | | | | | | | | | | |

Okay, Nick, count. Count right.

One, two, three, four, five, six, seven, eight, nine, ten, eleven, twelve. Draw a circle around them. Okay, now, one, two, three, four, five, six, seven. Draw a circle around those. Now what?

Think, Nick, think. Now what do I do, Mrs. Gordon? Now what do I do, Mom? Think, Nick! But it hurts so much to think. What do I do, Jesus?

What? Oh, yeah! Count them all! Count them all! Count all the sticks I circled! One, two, three, four, five, six, seven, eight, nine, ten, eleven, twelve, thirteen, fourteen, fifteen, sixteen, seventeen, eighteen, nineteen. NINETEEN! 12 + 7 = 19! 19! I did it!

"Nick, I can help you now," Mrs. Gordon said.

"That's okay, I did it. I finished my math. But can I take a ball out for recess? I need to kick it up 19 feet into the sky so Jesus can see it!"

Sabotage in Space

Can you save the Stargate *in time?*

by Ray Seldomridge

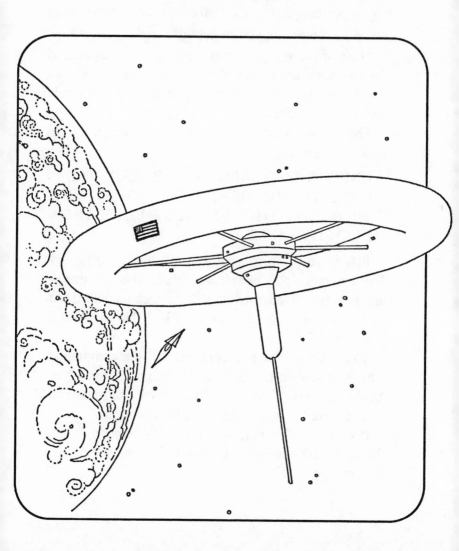

SABOTAGE IN SPACE

The job sounded exciting to you at first—being a communications assistant aboard the space station *Stargate*. And few young people ever get such a training opportunity. But after only five days of watching the Vidtext monitor, you're getting bored.

Most of the bulletins coming in from Houston and the moon are too technical to interest you, or too routine to require special handling. You wish you could just get up and explore this amazing space station.

The evening drags on. Suddenly, the screen flashes another message:

UNIDENTIFIED SABOTEUR ABOARD STARGATE. FUSION DEVICE SET TO GO OFF MIDNIGHT 1/1/2050. MUST FIND AND DESTROY.—HOUSTON.

Just as you leap to your feet, all the lights go out. The Vidtext display goes blank. It's another power failure, but short-lived; the lights come back on within seconds. The message, however, is lost. No printout is possible.

You jump on the intercom and tell the commander what you saw on the monitor. He laughs! "Just a New Year's Eve joke?" he suggests. "Or the wild imagination of a tired young communications assistant?"

It's only two hours to midnight. No one but you (and the saboteur) knows of the bomb. You must find and disarm it yourself.

If you head for the Storage Room, *go to 5*. If you ascend to Station Control, *go to 14*.

1 "Hey, how's it going?" calls a crew member as you enter.

"Not so good," you reply, trying to explain the emergency facing the *Stargate*. Several off-duty personnel listen to your story, but they all think it's funny. Sipping their coffee, they go back to talking excitedly about how humanity's leap to the stars is part of the "evolutionary development of the species." It's your turn to laugh; you tell them the only real "development" worth discussing is the promised Second Coming.

If you try the Observatory, *go to 13*. If you aim for the Life Search Lab, *go to 7*.

2 The center is humming with activity. White-coated technicians are experimenting to see how microgravity affects the manufacture of anti-cancer medicines, high-strength alloys and temperature-resistant glass.

You begin to ask one of them about a bomb, when suddenly an alarm sounds. A test tube has broken, releasing a cancer virus into the air. Quickly you escape before the quarantine doors automatically shut. (You were the only one without a mask.) Do you go to the Greenhouse? *See 4*. Do you try the Gift Shop? *Go to 16*.

3 Heading down a long corridor toward the hub of the space station, you begin to float in the air. You arrive at the zero-gravity gym and clip your safety line to one of the railings so you can watch the game. In this so-called "orbit basketball," dribbling is allowed against all six walls (including the "ceiling" and "floor"). The helmeted players dart up, down and around like guppies in an aquarium, careful not to crash too hard into the walls. The women's team is leading the men's by 20 points.

There's no place to hide a bomb in this gym, so you find the exit and head toward the Education Unit. *Go to 19.*

4 The greenhouse employs the latest soil-free tech-nology to grow vegetables and other plants without pests or disease. Under the lights are rows and rows of cucumbers, tomatoes, peas, lettuce, strawberries, herbs and even oats—all nearly ready for the crew's table.

A ticking sound makes you tense up; then you real-ize it is only the timer for the lights. Do you head for the Docking Bay? *Go to 10.* Do you try the Gift Shop? *Go to 16.*

5 Rows of high shelves fill this dimly lit room. You glance at one carton labeled "SHORT-SLEEVED, SIZE 34." These are disposable paper clothes, which everyone wears. Water aboard *Stargate* is too precious to waste on washing clothes. On the next shelf are boxes of sunglasses, rolls of Velcro tape and first-aid supplies.

If the fusion device is here, it would take days to find. And you don't *have* days, so you move on. If you head for the Solar Collection Terminal, *go to 11*. If you try the Habitat, *go to 18*.

6 Who would have expected to see this small park—complete with trees, grass, picnic tables and a flowing stream—in the middle of a space station? Planners wisely included it when they realized people cannot live for long in a world of metal, plastic and humming machines.

On earth, conditions are becoming desperate, with mega-cities eating up available nature spots around them. Even a park like this—with the silence and peace it offers—is getting hard to find there.

You say a prayer of thanks for God's creation before moving on. Do you try the Education Unit? *Go to 19.* Or the Physics Lab? *Go to 12.*

7 Radio telescopes in this lab are listening for even the faintest broadcast signals from life-forms elsewhere in the galaxy. None have been heard yet. Scientists claim the laws of probability *prove* there must be life on other planets. But as a Christian, you know it's not a question of probability, but simply of what God has chosen to create.

Finding no fusion device, you choose between the Observatory (*go to 13*) and the Materials Processing Center (*go to 2*).

8 Big bang indeed! Here's the fusion device ticking away in the hollowed-out book. It's already 11:50 p.m., so you race back to the Docking Bay, place the bomb in a repair shuttle, and auto-launch the spacecraft out into the heavens where the explosion will never even be heard.

With God's help, the new year is going to be a good one!

9 It's "Film Classics Night" at the theater. Movies featured include the memorable *Indiana Jones Jr. and the Mountains of Mars, Star Trek XXIV (The Tenth Generation)* and *Ernest Goes to the Sun.*

It seems a hopeless task to locate a bomb in a dark theater, so you give up. Do you try the Library? *Go to 17.* Or the Hospital? *Go to 20.*

10 Passengers from the latest aeroshuttle flight are streaming into the bay. They've paid a high price to join in the annual "New Year's Eve Party in Space." You hear a tour guide explaining, "*Stargate*'s crew of 175 works and lives comfortably in this doughnut-shaped station, which has a diameter of 200 feet. Assignments last from six to nine months, depending on—"

It's fun to watch these newcomers bounce around helplessly in low gravity, but you must hurry. Do you set off for the Gym (*go to 3*) or the Education Unit (*go to 19*)?

11 Deflected by mirrors, sunlight strikes vast solar-cell panels on *Stargate*; then in this terminal, the energy is converted into microwaves that are beamed down to earth. You've been told that most of Angeldiego (formerly Los Angeles and San Diego, now all one city) depends on this terminal for its power.

Could the saboteur, you wonder, *be out to destroy Southern California, not just the space station?* In either case, there's no sign of a bomb. If you proceed to the Cafe/Lounge, *go to 1*. If you try the Habitat, *go to 18*.

12 Even on New Year's Eve, two physicists are busy monitoring the Nintendo mainframe computer. One of them, Dr. Amos Quark, recently proved that black holes don't exist. He also just published findings that show the entire universe (not just the sun) will someday end. This study has caused quite a stir in scientific circles, but it didn't surprise you a bit. As Jesus once said, "Heaven and earth will pass away. . . ."

Everything seems normal here. Do you move on to the Theater (*go to 9*) or the Hospital (*go to 20*)?

13 No one is seated in the dozen swivel-mounted chairs near the long window. Stopping for a moment, you are astounded again at the sight: Thousands of stars glisten in the black expanse, while a portion of the earth is moving in from the left. Only

25,000 miles away, the enormous planet is brilliant; you'll need sunglasses to view any more of it. Despite a brownish cloud cover, the earth is still a beautiful sight. You're reminded of Psalm 8—"When I consider the heavens, . . . what is man?"—and realize God will help you through this present crisis.

Want to try the Greenhouse? *Go to 4.* Or the Materials Processing Center? *Go to 2.*

14 This, you realize, would be a logical place to plant a bomb. For here are the controls that regulate all of *Stargate's* vital functions: air pressure, temperature, power distribution and—most important—the extra-vehicular rockets used to speed up or slow down *Stargate's* rotation. Stopping the spin would eliminate the centrifugally-induced microgravity, making everything—and everybody—weightless. If this happened without warning, serious injury or death could result.

The captain on duty says all is in order, so you decide to look elsewhere. If you try the Solar Collection Terminal, *go to 11.* For the Storage Room, *go to 5.*

15 It's a funny book, but you've already seen most of these cartoons in the *Stargazette* newspaper. You put the book down and pick up *Happy Accidents. Go to 21.*

16 Lots of tourists are milling about the store, buying coffee mugs and paper sweatshirts that carry the *Stargate* emblem. This does not seem a likely place for sabotage, so you prepare to leave. On your way out, you pick up a copy of the latest 120-page *Clubhouse* magazine.

Do you try the Park? *Go to 6.* Or do you head for the Docking Bay? *Go to 10.*

17 You start to search for a bomb among the shelves. But your attention is sidetracked by several interesting new books. Do you pick up *The Far Side of the Moon* by Gary Larson III? Then *go to 15.* Or a book on the *Origins of the Big Bang? Go to 8.* Or another volume called *Happy Accidents? Go to 21.*

18 Here, in the crew's living quarters, everyone seems to be either sleeping or watching TV. One big screen is tuned to the Titanium Bowl game between Caltech and Rensselaer. Another has a news show on "Fifty Years in Review," and a third has a science special on moon mining. But all eyes are on the football. It seems that Caltech has just scored their first touchdown in nearly a hundred years, so everyone's too excited to talk to you. Do you move on to the Life Search Lab? *Go to 7.* Or to the Cafe/Lounge? *Go to 1.*

19 At this late hour, of course, no class is in session. But while searching for a fusion device, you pause and flip through a textbook on the teacher's desk. It's all about the importance of moral values, with chapters on honesty, fairness, kindness, and so on. The book's preface says "humankind has learned the hard way that society cannot survive without moral values." *If they only knew,* you reflect, *where those "values" came from in the first place—the Bible!*

Do you decide to try the Physics Lab? *Go to 12.* Do you want to check out the Theater? *Go to 9.*

20 The first thing you see is a drooling newborn baby in the maternity ward window. Incredible! And so cute! You realize you've *got* to find that bomb, if for no other reason than to save this one, precious new life. You charge ahead to the Library. *Go to 17.*

21 Oh, no, not another book on evolution! Right away, you recognize more of the same lame-brain arguments and phony science that they've been trying to sell to the public for a century. You decide to try *Origins of the Big Bang* instead. *Go to 8.*